JULIA DE

JULIA DE ROUBIGNÉ

by

HENRY MACKENZIE

Edited
& with an Introduction
by SUSAN MANNING

TUCKWELL PRESS

This edition published in 1999 by

Tuckwell Press Ltd
The Mill House
Phantassie
East Linton
East Lothian EH40 3DG

Introduction and Notes
Copyright © 1999 Susan Manning

ISBN 1 86232 047 0

The publishers acknowledge subsidy from
the Scottish Arts Council
towards the publication of this volume

A Catalogue record for this book
is available on request from the
British Library

Set in ITC Founder's Caslon 12 by JHtyp., Rushden
Printed and bound by Cromwell Press,
Trowbridge, Wiltshire

CONTENTS

INTRODUCTION

HENRY MACKENZIE's third and last novel was one of the better-known works to emerge in the wake of Rousseau's *succès de scandale, Julie, ou la nouvelle Héloïse*, in the final quarter of the eighteenth century. Immediately popular with contemporaries, it seems nonetheless to have been something of a 'novelist's novel', and has fared poorly since compared with the briefer, less complex *Man of Feeling* (1771), which caught — and indeed directed — the mood of an entire generation before becoming a historical curiosity interesting mainly to students of the cult of sensibility. Although (as this introduction will suggest) *Julia de Roubigné* offers both a more extended and reflective consideration of sensibility than the earlier novel, and a subtler understanding of the processes by which a mind comes to disorder, it has scarcely caught the attention of twentieth-century readers and critics. This edition aims to draw new readers to Mackenzie's compelling final experiment in fiction.

Mackenzie's novels play, in what seems to us now a very modern way, with the conditions of their own fictionality and authorship. In the opening pages of *The Man of Feeling*, the narrator retrieves a fragmentary manuscript from a curate who is tearing it up to supply wadding for his gun. Affecting to disparage the tale he is about to present to the reader, the narrator laments that mutilation has lessened its emotional power by depriving the manuscript of authorship:

had the name of a Marmontel, or a Richardson, been on the title-page —
'tis odds I should have wept.

But

One is ashamed to be pleased with the works of one knows not whom.[1]

Mackenzie, who composed *The Man of Feeling* while a young Scottish lawyer training in London, was making a graceful joke out of his unknownness as an author and covering his tracks at the same time by a nonchalant refusal to 'own' the work. If his audience failed to be moved by his tale, their insensibility had been anticipated in the text by the narrator himself. Doing this, however, he was also doing more, and the authorities he invokes are significant. The names of Jean François Marmontel (1723– 1799), popular French writer of *Contes Moraux* or moral tales, and Samuel Richardson, author of the undisputed masterpiece of educative sensibility, *Clarissa* (1747–48), at once give an imagined reader clear directions as to *how* — according to what conventions of taste — the ensuing narrative should be read, and (though more indirectly) point to a crucial feature of the 'cult of Sensibility': that the emotional effect is neither spontaneous nor intuitive, but conditioned by a complex series of expectations.[2]

Born in 1745, the year of the Jacobite rebellion, to a well-known Edinburgh lawyer and a Highland gentlewoman, and educated in Edinburgh in the 1760s, Mackenzie grew up with the ambiguous consequences of the cult of sensibility. He knew most of the great figures of the Scottish Enlightenment, including John Home (the author of *Douglas*, a Scottish dramatic *cause célèbre*), the historian William Robertson, Hugh Blair, and the philosophers and rhetoricians Adam Ferguson, David Hume and Adam Smith (to

---

1. *The Man of Feeling*, *The Works of Henry Mackenzie* (1808), with a new Introduction by Susan Manning (London: Routledge / Thommes Press, 1996), I, 6. Subsequent references (other than to *Julia de Roubigné*, where page numbers refer to the present edition) to works by Mackenzie will be to this edition.

2. There is a large secondary literature on the eighteenth-century literature of Sensibility. See, for example, Janet Todd, *Sensibility: An Introduction* (London: Methuen, 1986), and John Mullen, *Sentiment and Sociability: The Language of Feeling in the Eighteenth Century* (Oxford: Clarendon Press, 1988).

whom he referred as 'my friend').[3] He subsequently made use of his wide range of contacts as editor of (and chief contributor to) *The Mirror* (1779–80) and *The Lounger* (1785–87), influential periodicals in the style of Addison's *Spectator*, which helped to establish the cultural credentials of Edinburgh as 'the Athens of the North'. Widely regarded as the elder statesman of enlightened literary society in Scotland, Mackenzie encouraged young authors — notably the near-destitute Robert Burns, whose *Poems, Chiefly in the Scottish Dialect* he praised in a famous *Lounger* essay of 1786, and thereby prevented the emigration of the poet. He was not only an astute promoter of the literary talents of others, but presciently open to literary developments in a wider arena. His 'Essay on the German Theatre' presented to the Royal Society of Edinburgh in 1988 was of crucial importance in alerting British writers to proto-Romantic movements in Europe. This essay stimulated the young Walter Scott's interest in German literature: he went on to read widely and to translate Bürger's *Lenore* and *Wild Huntsman* for British audiences.

It is ironic, therefore, that Mackenzie's literary reputation has since been identified with his first excessively sympathetic protagonist, who earned him the soubriquet 'the Man of Feeling', for (so I suggest) his work as a whole is less an endorsement than a sceptical inquiry into the conditions and effects of sentiment on human behaviour. When contemporaries used the term of him, however, they did so with a full sense of irony: Mackenzie was a product of the Scottish Enlightenment, socially and professionally active and effective as lawyer and man of letters, 'alert as a contracting tailor's needle in every sort of business', as Walter Scott affectionately described him.[4] So we should be careful — returning to the issue of 'authority' — of identifying his own

---

3. Mackenzie attempted unsuccessfully to persuade Smith to write for *The Mirror*, according to Smith's biographer. See I. S. Ross, *The Life of Adam Smith* (Oxford: Clarendon Press, 1995), p. 343.

4. *The Journal of Sir Walter Scott*, ed. W. E. K. Anderson (Oxford: Clarendon Press, 1972), p. 26.

point of view too directly with the sentimental quintessences of his protagonists.

On 27 January 1777, Mackenzie wrote to his cousin Elizabeth Rose, 'Among other Employments is that of giving to the Public a Story which I had sketch'd out some Time ago, & had Leisure, during my Confinement last Spring, to resume. It is, probably, the last of the Kind which other Labours will allow me to lay before the World'.[5] The previous year he married a distant kinswoman, Penuel Grant. The marriage seems to have been both prudent and successful: to his friend Nancy Ord, he wrote in October 1775 that 'I think we have each other's Hearts so well, that the closest Connexion cannot unfold in them a Disguise to either'.[6] No potential for sentimental misunderstandings here. In the fullness of time their union would be blessed by fourteen children, and there is no evidence for a biographical link between Mackenzie's own happy marriage and the story of the fatal one which he began to compose so soon thereafter. And yet the conjunction is, at least, suggestive, and is implicit in the reading of the novel offered below.[7]

The 'editor' of *Julia de Roubigné* (who is not to be confused with Mackenzie himself) presents a little prefatory fiction of discovery and transmission analogous to that of *The Man of Feeling*, to intro-

5. *Letters to Elizabeth Rose of Kilravock on Literature, Events and People* 1768–1815, ed. Horst Drescher (Münster, 1987), pp. 198–99.

6. *Literature and Literati: The Literary Correspondence and Notebooks of Henry Mackenzie, Vol.* 1: *Letters* 1766–1827 ed. Horst Drescher (Frankfurt am Main: Verlag Peter Lang, 1989), p. 71.

7. The letter to Elizabeth Rose in which he announces *Julia de Roubigné* also discusses the matrimonial problems of a mutual acquaintance, and makes clear Mackenzie's view that women are often led 'astray' either by a 'fastidious Nicety which cannot be pleased at all, or th[e] Delusion which is self-pleased without the Allowance of Rea[son] or of Prudence; and if once the romantic Disposition has fairly pictured its Man, the Admonition of Parents, the Advice of Friends, & the Opinion of the World, do but serve to heighten the Colouring'. He was obviously thinking seriously about such issues at a more general level around the time of *Julia*'s composition.

duce a tale that has gratified his own melancholy sensibilities: having translated and edited the papers given to him by a Frenchman, 'I found it a difficult task to reduce them into narrative, because they are made up of sentiment, which narrative would destroy' (p. 5). Form and feeling are intimately connected. Fictional letters were a favoured device of mid-eighteenth-century literature for several reasons, the most obvious being that their illusion of immediacy seemed the appropriate vehicle for the unmediated expression of personal feelings. Drama and emotional tension were created by the epistolary interactions of various correspondents. Pointing his reader's attention so particularly to the fictional convention in the Preface, Mackenzie was advertising *Julia*'s connection with the highly successful — if also controversial — strain of sentimental fiction, whose most influential, and most provocative, exemplar was Rousseau's *Julie, ou La Nouvelle Héloïse* (1761). The congruence of names is clearly no accident.

What of the emotional letters whose presentation was so carefully stage-managed for maximum sentimental effect? Moving from the Preface to the body of the story, a certain stiltedness in the exalted accents of the protagonists is immediately noticeable. Their letters seem in many cases to express a kind of prefabricated sentiment. Idiomatic realism is clearly not at the heart of the book's purpose; but nor is there any evidence, internal or external, to suggest that the work is intended as a straight satire on sentimental excess. Mackenzie has mastered the mannerisms of a literary form at its point of decadence, and the question is really whether *Julia de Roubigné* represents the expiring breath of a tradition in the novel stretching back at least to *Clarissa*, or whether this unique compression of oppositional voices into expressions of emotional states in the protagonists may not rather have pointed the novel, particularly in Scotland, into new ways of rendering psychological disturbance.

Walter Scott (who dedicated his first Scottish novel, *Waverley*, to Mackenzie in 1814), for one, saw nothing secondhand or tired in his contemporary's writing: 'His works possess the rare and invaluable property of originality, to which all other qualities are as dust in the balance,' Scott wrote as late as 1823.[8] If we accept that the correspondents in *Julia de Roubigné* are not so much characters as they are counters in an ethical and aesthetic debate, it is possible to suggest that it may be best read as a sceptical inquiry, at once very much a product of its time, and not bound by the limitations of any single train of thought. Readers have often been tempted to see a division between Mackenzie the sentimental novelist, author of the hugely popular *Man of Feeling* and the impeccably tragic *Julia de Roubigné*, and Mackenzie the moral essayist, literary preceptor and public figure, whose writing cautions against excessive indulgence of feeling and the neglect of reason. But the division may be less real than apparent.

The best clue to Mackenzie's intentions in undertaking *Julia* comes from Scott, who wrote a brief introduction to his life and works for Ballantyne's Novelists' Library in 1823. Here he describes the seeds of the novel germinating in a conversation between the novelist and Henry Home, Lord Kames, in which the latter commented on how most poems, plays and novels spring from the machinations of some malevolent character. In response, Scott says,

the author undertook ... the composition of a story, in which the characters should be all naturally virtuous, and where the calamities of the catastrophe should arise ... not out of schemes of premeditated villany [sic], but from the excess and over-indulgence of passions and feelings, in themselves blameless, nay, praiseworthy, but which, encouraged to a morbid excess, and coming into fatal though fortuitous concourse with each other, lead to the most disastrous consequences.[9]

Further evidence that *Julia de Roubigné*, in other words, was an experiment, an inquiry into what — 'villany' aside — could propel

---

8. 'Henry Mackenzie', in *Lives of the British Novelists*, vol. 1; reprinted in Ioan Williams, ed., *Sir Walter Scott on Novelists and Fiction* (London: Routledge & Kegan Paul, Ltd., 1968), p. 77.

9. *Ibid.*, p. 81.

virtuous characters into disaster. The characters are all high-prin-
cipled, and well-intentioned; being human, they are also weak, and
their weakness, as Scott makes clear, is to become victims of their
own sensibilities, their own exclusive reliance on the dictates of
the emotions. There is thus no need of an Iago, no call for a
dropped handkerchief, in this eighteenth-century tragedy of
jealousy. Marmontel is not directly mentioned in *Julia*, but the
work contains many traces of Mackenzie's continuing interest in
the French author of the *Moral Tales*. (Even the name of the
French count may be borrowed from the Montauban Academy,
which awarded Marmontel a silver lyre for his poetry and thereby
sent him from the provinces to Paris to pursue a literary career.)
More intrinsic to the inquiry of Mackenzie's narrative, however,
is Marmontel's practice of articulating virtuous emotions in his
characters with a complete absence of either reticence or irony, both
of which appear to a modern reader necessary to avoid embarrassment. But this moral 'language' (as Mackenzie would refer to it in
his *Lounger* essays), characteristic of a fairly unchallenging version
of 'sentiment', gives way in the latter half of the novel to a very
different kind of idiom, which moves the reader onto quite a
different plane of psychological intensity.

Julia is not only a dependent daughter; through her mother's
untimely death she is deprived of vital parental guidance and
sympathy in the matter of matrimony: motherless daughters are
inevitably vulnerable to exploitation or corruption in the culture
of the novel. Moreover, as the innocent object of the wealthy
Count de Montauban's admiration, she becomes unwillingly
implicated in her father's financial survival. In making the decision
whether or not to marry her father's benefactor, she in effect
chooses either to be the saviour of his honour and financial probity
or the agent of his downfall. Her choice is therefore no choice at
all, as Mackenzie makes clear, its grounds are all predetermined
by the actions and wishes of others. In acceding to Montauban's
and her father's wishes, she knowingly violates her own feelings
— always a source of disaster in the literature of sensibility. In this

sense, poor Julia has all the cards stacked against her: Mackenzie builds the walls of her dilemma with calculating precision. As a virtuous and dutiful daughter she silences the protests of the 'voice within' before the needs of a desperate father and a proud and powerful suitor.

The episodes in Savillon's history which take place in the American colonies, though not directly connected with the main events of the novel, link to its narrative of sentiment through their meditation on slavery, ownership and freedom.[10] Savillon's enlightened treatment of the slave Yambu is in striking contrast to both Roubigné's and Montauban's proprietorial attitudes to the disposal of Julia's affections, her future, and her body ('This bosom is the property of Montauban' (p. 132), she announces darkly to Maria).[11] The reality of the moral dilemma is unquestionable, but Mackenzie seems to suggest that, despite the unpropitious circumstances, victim status *is* in some senses chosen — if only in the *nature* of the response to an adverse situation: reason may provide at least some measure of free will, whereas the realm of sensibility is not only a passive and reactive one, but ultimately very destructive for the individual. In some ways, though their cases are not really comparable, Julia has a less 'free' *mind* than Yambu.

In an essay for his periodical *The Lounger*, Mackenzie wrote a measured defence of novel-writing and reading, in which (while generally approving their moral effect on readers) he identified 'the principal danger of novels, as forming a mistaken and pernicious system of morality' to arise from 'that war of duties which is to be found in so many of them, particularly in that species called the sentimental'. This he located specifically with 'our neighbours the French'

---

10. Once again, on the issue of slavery Mackenzie's thinking is very much of — or in this case in advance of — his time. See note to p. 96, below.

11. David Marshall makes this point in 'The Business of Tragedy: Accounting for Sentiment in *Julia de Roubigné*, in *Passionate Encounters in a Time of Sensibility*, eds. Maximillian Novak and Anne Mellor (Maryland: University of Delaware Press, 1999).

whose style of manners, and the very powers of whose language, give them a great advantage in the delineation of that nicety, that subtilty of feeling, those entanglements of delicacy, which are so much interwoven with the characters and conduct of the chief personages ... The duty to parents is contrasted with the ties of friendship and of love; the virtues of justice, of prudence, of economy, are put in competition with the exertions of generosity, of benevolence, and of compassion: and even of these virtues of sentiment there are still more refined divisions, in which the overstrained delicacy of the persons represented always leads them to act from the motive least obvious, and therefore generally the least reasonable.[12]

This might stand as an extraordinarily apt critique of the dilemmas of his own protagonists in *Julia de Roubigné*: a French heroine of unusual sensibility forced by a sense of duty and obligation to her father to marry a man she does not love and thereby to deny her early, enduring love and friendship for another man; a suitor whose benevolence and compassion cannot be separated, even in his own mind, from his manoeuvre to acquire a virtuous woman as his wife. The essay continues:

In the enthusiasm of sentiment there is much the same danger as in the enthusiasm of religion, of substituting certain impulses and feelings of what may be called a visionary kind, in the place of real practical duties, which in morals, as in theology, we might not improperly denominate good works.

How should a man holding these views, as Mackenzie apparently consistently did, have published, in all seriousness, this domestic tragedy of sentiment in which virtuous and well-intentioned characters are so overborne by their emotional responses that they succumb, on the one hand, to an ambivalent and clandestine meeting with a former lover, and on the other, to murderous jealousy? What kind of 'inquiry' is this? A further look at the ambiguities of 'sentiment', and at Mackenzie's carefully distanced presentation of his narrative, may help.

---

12. *Works*, VI, p. 181.

I have suggested above that in both *The Man of Feeling* and *Julia de Roubigné* the self-conscious prefatory fictions of transmission alert the reader to a mood of 'sensibility' or 'sentiment' in which — for best 'effect' (another crucial term) — the ensuing tales should be read.[13] Both terms have to do with the 'authority' of subjectively experienced emotions, and the possibility or the value of conveying these to another person. The primary authority of any emotion comes from the fact that it is directly experienced by an individual: another person may question the justice or the appropriateness of that feeling, but may not deny its existence. Mackenzie's novels attempt to find a literary medium to investigate the experience — and the effects — of such unchallenged emotional primacy on the lives of individuals. There is a precise philosophical background to his inquiry, and it is to this that we must now turn.

Mid-eighteenth century moral philosophers, following the lead of Francis Hutcheson and Anthony Ashley, first Earl of Shaftesbury, developed a theory of moral behaviour founded in ideas of natural benevolence. The principal exponent of what became known as the 'Scottish school' was the philosopher Adam Smith, whose *Theory of Moral Sentiments* (1759) contended that the ethical response of an impartial observer to any event arises from a natural and irresistible sympathetic inclination towards a virtuous action, and a corresponding aversion from a vicious one. So a noble deed excites the desire of emulation in an observer, while the spectacle of an abandoned child will command sympathy towards the

---

13. 'Sensibility' and 'sentiment' are not interchangeable terms in eighteenth-century aesthetics, as Jerome McGann points out in *The Poetics of Sensibility: A Revolution in Literary Style* (Oxford: Clarendon Press, 1996). Broadly speaking, sensibility referred to a more instinctive, impulsive response, while sentiment was understood as a sophisticated form of understanding that characterised social interaction in civilised societies. Mackenzie, however, does not always make a clear distinction between the two terms.

infant's plight as experienced in its cries, and an aversion to the negligence of its guardian.

The ethics of sympathy itself derived from an understanding of human knowledge not (as had been held in the seventeenth century) as divinely implanted in the individual from birth or before, but as founded on perception and impression — on the experiences of the self, in short. This was the view of John Locke, whose *Essay on Human Understanding* (1698) proposes that we come into the world not as beings equipped with innate knowledge and capacities, but that all our knowledge is derived from perception, all our ideas the product of impressions of the world combined in the mind. The Scottish philosopher David Hume took Locke's challenge to rationalism to its logical, and (to contemporary ears) highly suspect, conclusion in *A Treatise of Human Nature* (1739–40), where he argued that *if* everything we know is the product of our own senses, the evidence of perception, then we can never be sure that we know anything beyond these sensory perceptions. The world, that is, may be a fiction of perception. 'This', as he famously put it, 'is the universe of the imagination, nor have we any idea but what is there produc'd.'[14]

Although Hume went on to write a subsequent treatise *On the Principles of Morals* along similar lines of sympathetic response to that of Adam Smith, the sceptical implications of his uncompromising epistemology place a question mark over what kind of objectivity or reality any impression or sensation of the world could ever claim. On the one hand, then, the evidence of the senses was absolute; on the other, it proved nothing beyond subjective impression. The 'authority' of experience, based on feeling, was open to question — but where was the authority by which it might be tried?

Metaphysicians and aestheticians circumvented the manifest dangers of epistemological scepticism: fragmentation of consensus into subjectivities whose trajectories of impression might never

---

14. *A Treatise of Human Nature*, ed. L. A. Selby-Bigge, second edn., text revised by Peter Nidditch (Oxford: Clarendon Press, 1978), p. 68.

meet, by posting an ideal, impartial spectator, the impeccability of whose responses would guarantee their objectivity and command assent from others. Herein lay Smith's 'impartial spectator', which he internalised to the conscience, the 'monitor' of all our actions, and Hume's figure of the man of taste whose perfect aesthetic responses could be the measure of others'.[15] The idea of 'authority' could take on a new, slightly different, but highly reassuring, meaning as the guarantor of 'right feeling'. In this sense, invoking the names of Richardson and Marmontel at the head of *The Man of Feeling* both claims a certain authority of sentimental response for the text to follow, and, because they are absent (the work is *not*, after all, by either author), suggests that not all the sentiments and sympathies it presents will be exemplary. As indeed the excessiveness of the sensibility of the protagonist Harley proves: he literally dies of too much feeling.

One of Mackenzie's own *Lounger* essays describes it as 'the business of tragedy to exhibit the passions, that is, the weaknesses of men'.[16] *Julia de Roubigné* is a domestic tragedy in two senses: its protagonists are — consonant with the social and family preoccupations of the *Mirror* / *Lounger* group (and also characteristic of the new German drama, in which Mackenzie was first becoming interested about this time) — of middling rather than courtly status. The novelist Anna Barbaud picked up on this aspect of the novel when she remarks that 'the scenes of domestic life and the affections which belong to them, are in many places beautifully touched; but an uniform hue of sadness pervades the whole. The sentiments are all pure, and the style exhibits fewer marks of imitation than [*The Man of Feeling*]'.[17] More

---

15. Adam Smith, *The Theory of Moral Sentiments* (1759), eds. D. D. Raphael and A. L. Macfie, The Glasgow Edition of the Works and Correspondence of Adam Smith, vol. 1 (Oxford: Oxford University Press, 1976, 1979), *e.g.* pp. 82–85; 128–32. Hume, 'Essay on the Standard of Taste', *Four Dissertations* (London, 1757). See also below, note to p. 146.

16. *Works*, V, p. 229.

17. *The British Novelists* (London, 1810), XXXIX, iii.

significantly to a modern reader, its passions too are privatised, as in the German plays whose novelty Mackenzie described as consisting 'chiefly in a minute development of feeling and sensibility; a refinement and eloquence of sentiment ... In sentiment, as in religion, there is a mystical sort of enthusiasm, which warms the fancy without submitting itself to the understanding; in sentiment, as in religion, enthusiasm is easily communicated'.[18] And the idiom is a great deal more varied and more challenging than 'an uniform hue of sadness' would seem to suggest. Walter Scott, who particularly admired *Julia de Roubigné*, described it as 'rather the history of effects produced on the human mind by a series of events, than the narrative of those events themselves'.[19] He saw it, that is, primarily as an interior drama, whose interest was played out within the minds of the protagonists.

It is characteristic of epistolary fictions — as of love letters — not only to convey the writer's own part, but to invent dialogues with the absent correspondent, and to imagine the effect of the letter on the reader. *Julia de Roubigné*, however, is unusual, if not unique, in its extension of this convention to the epistolary discourse of the whole novel: Mackenzie constructs the story so that there are literally *no* answering letters, no 'other' voices in the text not created in the imaginations of the protagonists — to the extent that it is perhaps more appropriate to describe its narrative form not as that of an epistolary novel, but rather as a series of dramatic monologues which, fatally, fail to converge in an agreed or shareable version of reality. All the letter writers (and this is most extremely true of Julia and Montauban) live within inturned imaginations which fail to register modifying contact with another viewpoint. Their story is not so much of betrayal as of self-betrayal, and its events are woven into the novel's narrative manner. In *Julia de Roubigné* Mackenzie re-writes for

18. 'Account of the German Theatre', *Transactions of the Royal Society of Edinburgh*, Vol. 1 (Edinburgh: J. Dickson & T. Cadell, 1788), pp. 164–65.
19. Scott, p. 80.

his time the observation of Shakespeare's Hamlet (a character to whose 'extreme sensibilities of mind' he devoted two whole *Mirror* essays) that 'there is nothing good or bad, but thinking makes it so'.[20]

Prior to her coerced marriage, and long before the fatal events begin to unfold, a Gothic strain of violation is in the air — or at least active in Julia's overheated imagination, and characterised by her excessive, disconnected expressions of terror. Her fears, in fact, precipitate the tragedy: she dare not confess her prior attachment to Savillon, and therefore escape marrying Montauban, because she 'shrinks' from her father's stern sense of honour, preferring instead to 'paint' 'images of vengeance and destruction' on her mind (p. 42). Her letters begin to embody a mental alienation and dissociation in which the absent confidante Maria becomes a strictly controlled *alter ego*. Because Maria's letters have no independent existence for the reader, but are present only in Julia's internalised redaction, their effectiveness is commuted into an additional form of self-expression for the distressed heroine, and the reader is deprived of whatever counsel they might have offered to avert the impending catastrophe: 'There is reason in this,' she addresses Maria, in response, apparently, to an objection of the latter, 'but while you argue from reason, I must decide from my feelings' (p. 57). The technique effects a kind of narrative separation of 'conscience' from 'feeling' in Julia's letters, when she imagines (within her own writing) Maria's response as the voice of conscience, calling her in a clear echo of Adam Smith 'my best monitor' (p. 77), 'my other conscience' (p. 66). Later, anxious to quell the guilt that rises in her, she writes, 'This one time I will silence the monitor within me' (p. 147). In another context, Mackenzie wrote sternly of just such a division in the writings of contemporary novelists of sentiment:

---

20. *Hamlet*, Act II, Scene ii, 11. 252–53; see *The Mirror*, nos. 99 & 100 (*Works*, IV, pp. 371–95).

This separation of conscience from feeling is a depravity of the most pernicious sort; it eludes the strongest obligation to rectitude, it blunts the strongest incitement to virtue; when the ties of the first bind the sentiment and not the will, and the rewards of the latter crown not the heart but the imagination.[21]

Like Maria for Julia, too, Montauban's correspondent Segarva is internally construed as an antagonist with whom he disputes: 'I have sometimes allowed myself to think, or rather I have supposed you thinking ...' (p. 71). Both protagonists, that is, 'voice' tempering or modifying thoughts without owning them; alternative possibilities seem to surface only to be subsumed in the self-destructive momentum of emotional response. This pre-emptive move creates a mannered, claustrophobic verbal environment in which the deadly logic of indulged sentiment works itself out unchecked by reference to any perception beyond the fatally compromised perspectives of the protagonists.

Read in this way, the strangely self-cancelling letters in this section of the novel accurately represent the turbulence in the minds of both Julia and Montauban, neither of whom is quite able to accept that things are as they seem, or willing to believe that they can be otherwise. Montauban's happiness cannot be complete until Segarva shares it; Julia declares that writing to Maria is 'only another sort of thinking' (p. 73). Neither Maria nor Segarva actually attends the union of Julia to Montauban; indeed, it is not too much to say that the nuptials are necessarily void as each party is primarily, and previously, engaged to its epistolary 'other self' with whom it sustains an inner dialogue that, dangerously, comes to replace the need for communication in the outer world.

To summarise, then: if these virtuous protagonists are un-witting agents in their own downfall, what is it that they do *not* do, that brings about their tragedy? Firstly, their marriage is

---

21. *Lounger* 20, Works, V, pp. 183–4.

fatally unsymmetrical: the passion of the one is reciprocated only by a reluctant sense of duty in the other; secondly, their relationship lacks frankness, and — implicitly — trust. Julia fears Montauban, and he misprises her and underestimates her fidelity. Thirdly, and most ominously, the narrative method shows just how completely they have allowed themselves to become alienated from the capacity to move properly outside their own emotional processes, so that they are unable to receive the vital checks and balances from others beyond their immediate situation. Self-deprived of the benefits of sociability, both are vulnerable to the chimeras of their terrorised imaginations.

In eighteenth-century Scottish social thought, conversation was not so much a polite accomplishment as a vital agent of ethical education, the balance which could measure, temper, and contain the excesses of individual sensibilities. The central figures in *Julia* are in conversation only with themselves, and nowhere more so than when their letters project the imaginary response of their correspondents. Not only correspondence but sociability itself is moribund in this novel which searches the psychological bankruptcies of sentimentalism. All the characters are either isolated by their own desire or by circumstances; the only one who repines at his condition is Savillon. Naturally sociable, he feels keenly the deprivation of his isolation from good companions in the colonies. But his attempt to enter the introverted hermetic world of self-enclosed emotions represented by Julia and Montauban is doomed from the beginning. Unable to open it up, he succeeds only in destroying it completely. There is, in truth, no meeting of minds in this novel, no 'sympathetic harmony' by which misunderstandings might be cleared and behaviour adjusted. Instead, Mackenzie seems to insist on disjunctions and failures which not only stress the isolation of the protagonists within their emotional worlds, but actually help to bring about the catastrophe. So, for example, there is the original failure of Julia and Savillon to speak clearly to one another of their feelings before the latter's departure to the New World, and, subsequently, there are the two antithetical accounts — Julia's and Montauban's — of the heroine being discovered with Savillon's portrait.

At another level, though, Julia's 'first and fatal indiscretion' — like that of her namesake the new Héloise — is the epistolary mode itself.[22] When, as a married woman, she enters into correspondence with Savillon, she renders her letters, and therefore her self, vulnerable to interception, to misinterpretation, and to violent reprisals. Reading his letters, she re-activates her desire for him: it is Julia herself who declares, 'in truth, my story is the story of sentiment' (p. 39). It might be argued that *this*, in fact, is the moment of Julia's 'fall': casting herself as sentimental heroine rather than virtuous wife, she begins to play that part in her letters and, ultimately, must suffer its fate of detection and revenge.

From this moment, the broken narratives of the letters take on a nightmare aspect. Their transmission is interrupted and confused: Montauban encloses sections of letters from Julia to Maria in his own missives to Segarva; his own diction is increasingly fragmented and incoherent, and both protagonist and victim (as Julia has now become) are afflicted by the bad dreams against which Montauban, like a latter-day Othello or Macbeth, finally cries desperately for 'some potion' (p. 162). The unstoppable effects of their capitulation to unchecked emotion are well described by Laurence Sterne's Walter Shandy when he observes that

— Love, you see, is not so much a SENTIMENT as a SITUATION, into which a man enters, as my brother *Toby* would do, into a corps — no matter whether he loves the service or no —[23]

If for 'love' we substitute its ugly underside 'jealousy', we have here a fair representation of what happens to Montauban in

22. The phrase is Nicola Watson's, in *Revolution and the Form of the British Novel, 1790–1825: Intercepted Letters, Interrupted Seductions* (Oxford: Clarendon Press, 1994), p. 12.

23. *The Life and Opinions of Tristram Shandy, Gentleman*, ed. Melvyn New & Joan New, 3 vols. (Gainesville: University Presses of Florida, 1978, 1984), 2:723.

Mackenzie's novel. Both love and jealousy, in the aesthetics of sensibility, are states of possession, of emotional abandonment where reason can no longer operate. The melodramatic final scenes of the novel seem less a glance back to Rousseau than a forward glimpse of James Hogg's Scottish masterpiece *The Confessions of a Justified Sinner* (1824), as Montauban, almost literally beside himself with jealousy, raves to Segarva:

Methought some one passed behind me in the room. I snatched up my sword in one hand, and a candle in the other. It was my own figure in the mirror that stood at my back. — What a look was mine! — Am I a murderer? — Justice cannot murder, and the vengeance of Montauban is just. (p. 157).

The quasi-Shakespearean elevation and excessive expressivity of Julia's and Montauban's diction in these final scenes are a measure of how far their emotions have become alienated from the moral 'language' of moderation and stoicism that Mackenzie's essays speak of. Having allowed their imaginations to deviate from this saving measure, there is no brake on events until the book, all passion spent, closes with a quasi-Shakespearean epilogue, spoken, Fortinbras-like, over the corpses of Montauban and Julia by M. de Rouillé, a new voice who enters the novel to salvage a rather questionable moral for the reader.

Some thoughts, it would seem, are better left unthought — and certainly unvoiced. Emotional expressiveness (so Mackenzie seems to suggest) has a momentum of its own, and may once set in train gather speed to fatal conclusions if not checked by reason at every point. The post-Romantic ideal of total emotional honesty was less obviously a natural desideratum to a writer of Mackenzie's era and background — indeed, it was liable to precipitate the individual who so indulged into uncontrollable areas of emotional experience inaccessible to the modifying responses of others. Two things, then, have gone wrong when Julia and Montauban write to Maria and Segarva as freely as to 'another self': firstly, both have lost the sense of the essential otherness of others, and the great value of this in stabilising a sense of self;

secondly, encouraged by this sense of a sympathetic *alter ego* within to speak of feelings well outwith the pale of normal decorum, they reap whirlwinds of uncontrollable emotional excess.

It is not to question either the success or the happiness of Mackenzie's own marriage to suggest a connection between this auspicious event and the far from felicitous outcome of the novel he undertook shortly thereafter. This is why I have chosen Henry Raeburn's portrait of Mrs William Urquhart (for which the subject probably sat shortly after her own marriage) as the cover picture for this edition. It catches to perfection the fragility of the young wife's composure, her dress and demeanour tensely beautiful with the sense of their own propriety. One guesses, looking at the careful quiescence of the mouth and the wistful, slightly distant look in the eyes, that it is a poise which might very easily be shaken by sentiment (whether in the form of novels or fashionable social affectation), and may only, according to the moderating stoical discourse of the *Mirror* and *Lounger*, be nurtured into stability by the good counsel of others.[24] Above all — to return to the novel — this young wife should avoid entering into sentimental correspondence of a clandestine kind, as Julia's mother makes clear in her neglected posthumous advice to her daughter:

beware of communicating to others any want of duty or tenderness she may think she has perceived in her husband. This untwists, at once, those delicate cords, which preserve the unity of the marriage-engagement. Its sacredness is broken for ever, if third parties are made witnesses of its failings, or umpires of its disputes (p. 82).

For if Mackenzie's meditations on what makes for happy married life led him (as there is evidence to suggest in both his

---

24. Raeburn painted most of the Mirror Club members: Mackenzie himself more than once, William Craig, Lord Abercromby, and Ballantyne, and his society paintings align themselves closely with the moral ethos of *The Mirror* and *The Lounger*. See Nicholas Phillipson, 'Manners, Morals and Characters: Henry Raeburn and the Scottish Enlightenment', in Duncan Thomson, ed., *The Art of Sir Henry Raeburn*, 1756–1823 (Edinburgh: Scottish National Portrait Gallery, 1997).

periodical essays and the letters of 1775–77) to believe that it is advisable to leave some avenues of passion — unmeasured longing for an impossible romantic deal, or extreme jealousy, for example — unexplored, what better exorcism for a prudent and ambitious young man than to cast them into an exemplary fiction where they might be at once expressed, disowned, and contribute to one of the great moral debates of his time?

It was a story told of Mackenzie that his wife shook her head sadly over him, chiding gently, 'Oh, Harry, Harry, your feeling is all on paper.'[25] Perhaps he knew enough to keep it there.

TEXTUAL NOTE

THE TEXT of *Julia de Roubigné* reprinted here is taken from volume III of Henry Mackenzie's *Works* (8 vols), collected and corrected by the author in 1808. That edition's 'Errata to Volume Third', which preface the volume, have been silently absorbed here. In two instances where obvious additional errata threaten to obscure the sense they have been corrected and indicated in the notes; otherwise eighteenth-century variations in spelling (and Mackenzie's own occasional idiosyncrasies) have been allowed to stand. Mackenzie's notes are indicated by asterisks, my own explanatory notes by superscript numerals.

Newnham College, Cambridge   SUSAN MANNING

---

25. Quoted by Harold W. Thompson, *A Scottish Man of Feeling* (London and New York: Oxford University Press, 1931), p. 181.

SELECTED BIBLIOGRAPHY

EDITIONS

The Works of Henry Mackenzie (1808), with a new Introduction by Susan Manning, 8 vols. (London: Routledge/ Thoemmes Press, 1996)

Mackenzie, Henry, *An Account of the Life and Writings of John Home*, with a new Introduction by Susan Manning, Lives of the Literati Series (Bristol: Thoemmes Press, 1997)

Mackenzie, Henry, *Letters to Elizabeth Rose of Kilravock, on Literature, Events and People, 1768–1815*, ed. Horst Drescher (Münster, 1987)

Literature and Literati: The Literary Correspondence and Notebooks of Henry Mackenzie, Vol. 1: Letters 1766–1827 ed. Horst Drescher (Frankfurt am Main: Verlag Peter Lang, 1989)

The Anecdotes and Egotisms of Henry Mackenzie, 1745–1831, ed. Harold W. Thompson (London, 1927)

BIOGRAPHY AND CRITICISM

Barker, Gerard A., *Henry Mackenzie* (Boston: Twayne Publishers, 1975)

Conger, Syndy McMillen, ed., *Sensibility in Transformation: Creative Resistance to Sentiment from the Augustans to the Romantics* (London and Toronto: Associated University Presses, 1990)

Duyfhuizen, Bernard, *Narratives of Transmission* (London and Toronto: Associated University Presses, 1992)

Dwyer, John, *Virtuous Discourse: Sensibility and Community in Late Eighteenth-Century Scotland* (Edinburgh: John Donald, 1987)

The Age of the Passions (East Linton: Tuckwell Press, 1998)

Garside, P. D., 'Henry Mackenzie, The Scottish Novel and *Blackwood's*

Magazine', *Scottish Literary Journal*, 15, no. 1 (May 1988), 25–48

[Lockhart, J. G.], *Peter's Letters to His Kinsfolk*, so-called '3rd edition', 3 vols. (Edinburgh and London, 1819)

McGann, Jerome, *The Poetics of Sensibility: A Revolution in Literary Style* (Oxford: Clarendon Press, 1996)

Mullan, John, *Sentiment and Sociability: The Language of Feeling in the Eighteenth Century* (Oxford: Clarendon Press, 1988)

Rousseau, Jean-Jacques, *Julie, or the New Eloise*, transl. Judith McDowell (University Park, Pennsylvania: Pennsylvania State University Press, 1968)

Scott, Walter, 'Henry Mackenzie', in *Lives of the Novelists*, The Complete Prose Works of Sir Walter Scott, 28 vols., vol. IV (Edinburgh: Cadell, 1834–36)

Smith, Adam, *The Theory of Moral Sentiments* (1759), eds. D. D. Raphael and A. L. Macfie, The Glasgow Edition of the Works and Correspondence of Adam Smith, vol. 1 (Oxford: Oxford University Press, 1976, 1979)

Thompson, Harold W., *A Scottish Man of Feeling* (London and New York: Oxford University Press, 1931)

Todd, Janet, *Sensibility: An Introduction* (London and New York: Methuen, 1986)

Tompkins, J. M. S., *The Popular Novel in England*, 1770–1800 (London, 1932, 1962)

Ware, Elaine, 'Charitable Actions Reevaluated in the Novels of Henry Mackenzie', *Studies in Scottish Literature*, XXXII (1987), 132–141

Warner, James H., 'Eighteenth-Century English Reactions to the *Nouvelle Héloise*', *Publications of the Modern Language Association* 52 ii (1937), 803–819

Watson, Nicola J., *Revolution and the Form of the British Novel*, 1790–1825: Intercepted Letters, Interrupted Seductions (Oxford: Clarendon Press, 1994)

JULIA DE ROUBIGNÉ:

A TALE,

IN

A SERIES OF LETTERS

INTRODUCTION

I HAVE formerly taken the liberty of holding some prefatory discourse with my readers, on the subject of those little histories which accident enabled me to lay before them.[1] This is probably the last time I shall make use of their indulgence; and, even if this Introduction should be found superfluous, it may claim their pardon, as the parting address of one, who has endeavoured to contribute to their entertainment.

I was favoured last summer with a visit from a gentleman, a native of France, with whose father I had been intimately acquainted when I was last in that country. I confess myself particularly delighted with an intercourse, which removes the barrier of national distinction, and gives to the inhabitants of the world the appearance of one common family. I received, therefore, this young Frenchman into that humble shed, which Providence has allowed my age to rest in, with peculiar satisfaction; and was rewarded, for any little attention I had in my power to shew him, by acquiring the friendship of one, whom I found to inherit all that paternal worth which had fixed my esteem, about a dozen years ago, at Paris. In truth, such attention always rewards itself; and, I believe, my own feelings, which I expressed to this amiable and accomplished Frenchman on his leaving England, are such as every one will own, whose mind is susceptible of feeling at all. He was profuse of thanks, to which my good offices had no title, but from the inclination that accompanied them — *Ici, Monsieur,* (said

---

1. Mackenzie's earlier novels *The Man of Feeling* (1771) and *The Man of the World* (1773).

3

I, for he had used a language more accommodated than ours to the lesser order of sentiments, and I answered him as well as long want of practice would allow me, in the same tongue,) — *Ici, Monsieur, obscur et inconnu, avec beaucoup de bienveillance, mais peu de pouvoir, je ne goûte pas d'un plaisir plus sincere, que de penser, qu'il y a, dans aucun coin du monde, un caeur honnête qui se souvient de moi avec reconnoissance.*

But I am talking of myself, when I should be giving an account of the following papers. This gentleman, discoursing with me on the subject of those letters, the substance of which I had formerly published under the title of the *Man of the World*, observed, that if the desire of searching into the records of private life were common, the discovery of such collections would cease to be wondered at. "We look," said he, "for the Histories of Men, among those of high rank; but memoirs of sentiment and suffering may be found in every condition.

"My father," continued my young friend, "made, since you saw him, an acquisition of that nature, by a whimsical accident. Standing one day at the door of a grocery-shop, making enquiry as to the lodgings of some person of his acquaintance, a little boy passed him, with a bundle of papers in his hand, which he offered for sale to the master of the shop, for the ordinary uses of his trade; but they differed about the price, and the boy was ready to depart, when my father desired a sight of the papers, saying to the lad with a smile, that, perhaps, he might deal with him for his book; upon reading a sentence or two, he found a style much above that of the ordinary manuscripts of a grocery-shop, and gave the boy his price at a venture, for the whole. When he got home, and examined the parcel, he found it to consist of letters put up, for the most part, according to their dates, which he committed to me, as having, he said, better eyes, and a keener curiosity, than his. I found them to contain a story in detail, which, I believe, would interest one of your turn of thinking a good deal. If you chuse to undergo the trouble of the perusal, I shall take care to have them sent over to you by the first opportunity I can find, and if you will do the Public the favour to digest them, as you did those of *Annesly* and his children," — My young Frenchman speaks the language of compliment; but I do not choose to translate any farther. It is enough to say, that I received his papers some time ago, and that they are those which I have translated, and now give to the world. I had, perhaps, treated them as I did the letters he mentioned; but I found it a difficult task to reduce them into narrative, because they are made up of sentiment, which narrative would destroy. The only power I have exercised over them, is that of omitting letters, and passages of letters, which seem to bear no relation to the story I mean to communicate. In doing this, however, I confess I have been cautious: I love myself (and am apt, therefore, from a common sort of weakness, to imagine that other people love) to read nature in her smallest character, and am often more apprised of the state of the mind, from very trifling, than from very important circumstances.

As, from age and situation, it is likely I shall address the public no more, I cannot avoid taking this opportunity of thanking it for the reception it has given to those humble pages which I formerly introduced to its notice. Unknown and unpatronized, I had little pretensions to its favour, and little expectation of it; writing, or arranging the writings of others, was to me only a favourite amusement, for which a man easily finds both time and apology. One advantage I drew from it, which the humane may hear with satisfaction; I often wandered from my own woe, in tracing the tale of another's affliction; and, at this moment, every sentence I write, I am but escaping a little farther from the pressure of sorrow.

Of the merit or faults of the composition, in the volumes of which I have directed the publication, a small share only was mine; for their tendency I hold myself entirely accountable, because, had it been a bad one, I had the power of suppressing them; and from their tendency, I believe, more than any other quality belonging to them, has the indulgence of their readers arisen. For that indulgence I desire to return them grateful acknowledgments as an editor; I shall be proud, with better reason, if there is nothing to be found in my publications, that may forfeit their esteem as a man.

Julia de Roubigné to Maria de Roncilles

"THE FRIENDSHIP of your Maria, misfortune can never deprive you of." — These were the words with which you sealed that attachment we had formed in the blissful period of infancy. The remembrance of those peaceful days we passed together in the convent, is often recalled to my mind, amidst the cares of the present. Yet do not think me foolish enough to complain of the want of those pleasures which affluence gave us; the situation of my father's affairs is such as to exclude luxury, but it allows happiness; and, were it not for the recollection of what he once possessed, which now and then intrudes itself upon him, he could scarce form a wish that were not gratified in the retreat he has found.

You were wont to call me the little philosopher; if it be philosophy to feel no violent distress from that change which the ill fortune of our family has made in its circumstances, I do not claim much merit from being that way a philosopher. From my earliest days I found myself unambitious of wealth or grandeur, contented with the enjoyment of sequestered life, and fearful of the dangers which attend an exalted station. It is therefore more properly a weakness, than a virtue, in me, to be satisfied with my present situation.

But, after all, my friend, what is it we have lost? We have exchanged the life of gaiety, of tumult, of pleasure they call it, which we led in Paris, when my father was a rich man, for the pure, the peaceful, the truly happy scenes, which this place affords us, now he is a poor one. Dependence and poverty alone are suffered to complain; but they know not how often greatness is dependent,

7

and wealth is poor. Formerly, even during the very short space of the year we were at Belville, it was vain to think of that domestic enjoyment I used to hope for in the country; we were people of too much consequence to be allowed the privilege of retirement, and, except those luxurious walks I sometimes found means to take — with you, my dear, I mean — the day was as little my own, as in the midst of our winter-hurry in town.

The loss of this momentous law-suit has brought us down to the level of tranquillity. Our days are not now pre-occupied by numberless engagements, nor our time anxiously divided for a rotation of amusements; I can walk, read, or think, without the officious interruption of polite visitors; and, instead of talking eternally of others, I find time to settle accounts with myself.

Could we but prevail on my father to think thus! — Alas! his mind is not formed for contracting into that narrow sphere, which his fortune has now marked out for him. He feels adversity a defeat, to which the vanquished submit, with pride in their looks, but anguish in their hearts. He is cut off from the enjoyment of his present state, while he puts himself under the cruel necessity of dissembling his regret for the loss of the former.

I can easily perceive how much my dearest mother is affected by this. I see her constantly on the watch for every word and look that may discover his feelings; and she has, too often, occasion to observe them unfavourable. She endeavours, and commonly succeeds in her endeavour, to put on the appearance of cheerfulness; she even tries to persuade herself, that she has reason to be contented; but, alas! an effort to be happy is always but an increase of our uneasiness.

And what is left for your Julia to do? In truth, I fear, I am of little service. My heart is too much interested in the scene, to allow me that command over myself, which would make me useful. My father often remarks, that I look grave; I smile, (foolishly I fear,) and deny it; it is, I believe, no more than I used to do formerly; but we were then in a situation that did not lead him to observe it. He had no consciousness in himself to prompt the observation.

How often do I wish for you, Maria, to assist me! There is something in that smile of yours, (I paint it to myself at this instant,) which care and sorrow are unable to withstand; besides the general effect produced by the intervention of a third person, in a society, the members of which are afraid to think of one another's thoughts. — Yet you need not answer this wish of mine; I know how impossible it is for you to come hither at present. Write to me as often as you can; you will not expect order in my letters, nor observe it in your answers; I will speak to you on paper when my heart is full, and you will answer me from the sympathy of yours.

LETTER II.

Julia to Maria

I AM to vex my Maria with an account of trifles, and those, too, unpleasant ones; but she has taught me to think, that nothing is insignificant to her, in which I am concerned, and insists on participating, at least, if she cannot alleviate my distresses.

I am every day more and more uneasy about the chagrin which our situation seems to give my father. A little incident has just now plunged him into a fit of melancholy, which all the attention of my mother, all the attempts at gaiety which your poor Julia is constrained to make, cannot dissipate or overcome.

Our old servant Le Blanc is your acquaintance; indeed he very soon becomes acquainted with every friend and visitor of the family; his age prompting him to talk, and giving him the privilege of talking.

Le Blanc had obtained permission, a few days since, to go on a visit to his daughter, who is married to a young fellow, serving in the capacity of coachman at a gentleman's in the neighbourhood of Belville. He returned last night, and, in his usual familiar manner, gave us an account of his expedition this morning.

My father enquired after his daughter; he gave some short answer as to her; but I could see by his face, that he was full of some other intelligence. He was standing behind my father, resting one hand on the back of his chair; he began to rub it violently, as if he would have given the wood a polish by the friction. "I was at Belville, Sir," said he. My father made no reply; but Le Blanc had got over the difficulty of beginning, and was too much occupied by the idea of the scene, to forbear attempting the picture.

"When I struck off the high road," said he, "to go down by the old avenue, I thought I had lost my way; there was not a tree to be seen. You may believe me as you please, Sir; but, I declare, I saw the rooks, that used to build there, in a great flock over my head, croaking, for all the world, as if they had been looking for the avenue too. Old Lasune's house, where you, Miss, (turning to me,) would frequently stop in your walks, was pulled down, except a single beam at one end, which now serves for a rubbing-post to some cattle that graze there; and your roan horse, Sir, which the marquis had of you in a present, when he purchased Belville, had been turned out to grass among the rest, it seems, for there he was, standing under the shade of the wall; and, when I came up, the poor beast knew me, as any Christian would, and came neighing up to my side, as he was wont to do. I gave him a piece of bread I had put in my pocket in the morning, and he followed me for more, till I reached the very gate of the house; I mean what was the gate when I knew it; for there is now a rail run across, with a small door, which Le Sauvre told me they call Chinese.[2] But, after all, the marquis is seldom there to enjoy these fine things; he lives in town, Le Sauvre says, eleven months in the year, and only comes down to Belville, for a few weeks, to get money to spend in Paris."

Here Le Blanc paused in his narration. I was afraid to look up to see its effect upon my father; indeed the picture which the poor fellow had, innocently, drawn, had too much affected myself. — Lasune's house! my Maria remembers it; but she knows not all the ties which its recollection has upon me.

I stole, however, a sidelong glance at my father. He seemed affected, but disdain was mixed with his tenderness; he gathered up his features, as it were to hide the effect of the recital. "You

2. The fashion for Chinoiserie, or Chinese-inspired interior and garden design, spread rapidly through France and Europe following Louis Le Vau's *Trianon de porcelaine* created for Louis XIV at Versailles. Montauban's installation of a 'Chinese' door at Belville indicates his wealth and status as a man of fashion at the Parisian court; Julia, bred in the country, is unfamiliar with these modish touches.

saw Le Sauvre then?" said he coolly. — "Yes," answered Le
Blanc; "but he is wonderfully altered since he was in your service,
Sir; when I first discovered him, he was in the garden, picking
some greens for his dinner; he looked so rueful when he lifted up
his head and saw me! indeed I was little better myself, when I cast
my eyes around. It was a sad sight to see! for the marquis keeps no
gardener, except Le Sauvre himself, who has fifty things to do
besides, and only hires another hand or two for the time he resides
at Belville in the summer. The walks, that used to be trimmed so
nicely, are covered with mole-hills; the hedges are full of great
holes, and Le Sauvre's chickens were basking in the flower-beds.
He took me into the house, and his wife seemed glad to see her old
acquaintance, and the children clambered up to kiss me, and Jeanot
asked me about his god-mother, meaning you, Madam; and his
little sister enquired after her handsome mistress, as she used to
call you, Miss. "I have got," said Nanette, "two new mistresses,
that are much finer drest than she, but they are much prouder,
and not half so pretty;" meaning two of the marquis's daughters,
who were at Belville for a few days, when their father was last
there. I smiled to hear the girl talk so, though, heaven knows, my
heart was sad. Only three of the rooms are furnished, in one of
which Le Sauvre and his family were sitting; the rest had their
windows darkened with cobwebs, and they echoed so when Le
Sauvre and I walked through them, that I shuddered, as if I had
been in a monument."

"It is enough, Le Blanc," said my mother in a sort of whisper.
My father asked some indifferent question about the weather. I
sat, I know not how, looking piteously, I suppose; for my mother
tapped my cheek with the word Child! emphatically pronounced.
I started out of my reverie, and finding myself unable to feign a
composure which I did not feel, walked out of the room to hide
my emotion. When I got to my own chamber, I felt the full force
of Le Blanc's description; but to me it was not painful: it is not on
hearts that yield the soonest that sorrow has the most powerful
effects; it was but giving way to a shower of tears, and I could

think of Belville with pleasure, even in the possession of another. — They may cut its trees, Maria, and alter its walks, but cannot so deface it as to leave no traces for the memory of your Julia: — Methinks I should hate to have been born in a town; when I say my native brook, or my native hill, I talk of friends of whom the remembrance warms my heart. To me, even to me, who have lost their acquaintance, there is something delightful in the melancholy recollection of their beauties; and, here, I often wander out to the top of a little broom-covered knoll, merely to look towards the quarter where Belville is situated.

It is otherwise with my father. On Le Blanc's recital he has brooded these three days. The effect it had on him is still visible in his countenance; and, but an hour ago, while my mother and I were talking of some other subject, in which he was joining by monosyllables, he said, all at once, that he had some thoughts of sending to the marquis for his roan horse again, since he did not chuse to keep him properly.

They, who have never known prosperity, can hardly be said to be unhappy; it is from the remembrance of joys which we have lost, that the arrows of affliction are pointed. Must we then tremble, my friend, in the possession of present pleasures, from the fear of their embittering futurity? or does Heaven thus teach us that sort of enjoyment, of which the remembrance is immortal? Does it point out those as the happy, who can look back on their past life, not as the chronicle of pleasure, but as the record of virtue?

Forgive my preaching; I have leisure and cause to preach. You know how faithfully, in every situation,

I am yours.

Julia to Maria

"I WILL speak to you on paper, when my heart is full." —
Misfortune thinks itself entitled to speak, and feels some consolation in the privilege of complaining, even where it has nothing to
hope from the utterance of complaint.

Is it a want of duty in me to mention the weakness of a parent?
Heaven knows the sincerity of the love I bear him! Were I
indifferent about my father, the state of his mind would not much
disquiet me; but my anxiety for his happiness carries me, perhaps,
a blameable length in that censure, which I cannot help feeling, of
his incapacity to enjoy it.

My mother too! if he knew how much it preys upon her gentle
soul, to see the impatience with which he suffers adversity! — Yet,
alas! unthinking creature that I am, I judge of his mind by my
own; and while I venture to blame his distress, I forget that it is
entitled to my pity.

This morning he was obliged to go to the neighbouring village
to meet a procureur from Paris on some business, which, he told
us, would detain him all day. The night was cold and stormy,
and my mother and I looked often earnestly out, thinking on the
disagreeable ride he would have on his return. "My poor
husband!" said my mother, as the wind howled in the lobby
beneath. "But I have heard him say, mamma, that, in these little
hardships, a man thinks himself unfortunate, but is never
unhappy; and you may remember he would always prefer riding
to being driven in a carriage, because of the enjoyment which, he
told us, he should feel from a clean room and a cheerful fire when
he got home." At the word *carriage*, I could observe my mother

sigh; I was sorry it had escaped me; but at the end of my speech, we looked both of us at the hearth, which I had swept but the moment before; the faggots were crackling in the fire, and my little Fidele lay asleep before it. — He pricked up his ears and barked, and we heard the trampling of horses in the court. "Your father is returned," cried my mother; and I ran to the door to receive him. "Julia, is it not?" said he, (for the servant had not time to fetch us a light;) but he said it coldly. I offered to help him off with his surtout. "Softly, child," said he, "you pull my arm awry." It was a trifle, but I felt my heart swell when he said this.

He entered the room; my mother took his hand in hers. "You are terribly cold, my love," said she, and she drew his chair nearer the fire; he threw aside his hat and whip, without speaking a word. In the centre of the table, which was covered for supper, I had placed a bowl of milk, dressed in a way I knew he liked, and had garnished it with some artificial flowers, in the manner we used to have our deserts done at Belville. He fixed his eyes on it, and I began to make ready my answer to a question I supposed he would ask, "who had trimmed it so nicely?" but he started hastily from his chair, and snatching up this little piece of ornament, threw it into the fire, saying, "We have now no title to finery." This was too much for me; it was foolish, very foolish, but I could not help letting fall some tears. He looked sternly at me; and muttering some words, which I could not hear, walked out of the room, and slapped the door roughly behind him. I threw myself on my mother's neck, and wept outright.

Our supper was silent and sullen; to me the more painful, from the mortifying reverse which I felt from what I had expected. My father did not taste the milk; my mother asked him to eat of it with an affected ease in her manner; but I observed her voice faulter as she asked him: As for me, I durst not look him in the face; I trembled every time the servant left the room: there was a protection, even in his presence, which I could not bear to lose. The table was scarcely uncovered, when my father said he was tired and sleepy; my mother laid hold of the opportunity, and offered to accompany him to their chamber: She bid me good-night; my father was silent; but I answered as if addressing myself to both.

Maria! in my hours of visionary indulgence, I have sometimes painted to myself a husband — no matter whom — comforting me amidst the distresses which fortune had laid upon us. I have smiled upon him through my tears; tears, not of anguish, but of tenderness; — our children were playing around us, unconscious of misfortune; we had taught them to be humble and to be happy; — our little shed was reserved to us, and their smiles to cheer it — I have imagined the luxury of such a scene, and affliction became a part of my dream of happiness.

━━

Thus far I had written last night; I found at last my body tired and drowsy, though my mind was ill disposed to obey it: I laid aside my pen, and thought of going to bed; but I continued sitting in my chair, for an hour after, in that state of languid thinking, which, though it has not strength enough to fasten on any single object, can wander without weariness over a thousand. The clock striking one, dissolved the enchantment; I was then with my Maria, and I went to bed but to continue my dream of her.

Why did I wake to anxiety and disquiet? — Selfish! that I should not bear, without murmuring, my proportion of both! — I met my mother in the parlour, with a smile of meekness and serenity on her countenance; she did not say a single word of last night's incident; and I saw she purposely avoided giving me any opportunity of mentioning it; such is the delicacy of her conduct with regard to my father. What an angel this woman is! Yet I fear, my friend, she is a very woman in her sufferings.

She was the only speaker of our company, while my father sat with us. He rode out soon after breakfast, and did not return till dinner-time. I was almost afraid of his return, and was happy to see, from my window, somebody riding down the lane along with him. This was a gentleman of considerable rank and fortune in our neighbourhood, the Count Louis de Montauban. I do not know how it has happened, but I cannot recollect having ever mentioned him to you before. He is not one of those very interesting characters, which are long present with the mind; yet his worth is universally acknowledged, and his friendship to my father, though of late acquisition, deserves more than ordinary acknowledgement from us. His history we heard from others, soon after our arrival here; since our acquaintance began, we have had it, at different times, from himself; for, though he has not much frankness about him to discover his secrets, he possesses a manly firmness, which does not shrink from the discovery.

His father was only brother to the late Francis Count de Montauban; his mother, the daughter of a noble family in Spain, died in childbed of him; and he was soon after deprived of his remaining parent, who was killed at a siege in Flanders. His uncle took, for some time, the charge of his education; but, before he attained the age of manhood, he discovered, in the count's behaviour, a want of that respect which should have distinguished the relation from the dependant; and after having, in vain, endeavoured to assert it, he took the resolution of leaving France, and travelled a-foot into Spain, where he met with a very kind reception from the relations of his mother. By their assistance, he was afterwards enabled to acquire a respectable rank in the Spanish army, and served, in a series of campaigns, with distinguished reputation. About a year ago, his uncle died unmarried; by this event he succeeded to the family estate, part of which is situated in this neighbourhood; and since that time, he has been generally here, employed in superintending it; for which, it seems, there was the greater necessity, as the late count, who commonly lived at the old hereditary seat of his ancestors, had, for some of the last years of his life, been entirely under the dominion of rapacious domestics, and suffered his affairs in this quarter to run, under their guidance, into the greatest confusion.

Though, in France, a man of fortune's residence at his country-seat is so unusual, that it might be supposed to enhance the value of such a neighbour, yet the circumstance of Montauban's great fortune was a reason, I believe, for my father shunning any advances towards his acquaintance.[3] The count at last contrived to introduce himself to us, (which, for what reason I know not, he seemed extremely anxious to do,) in a manner that flattered my father; not by offering favours, but by asking one. He had led a walk through a particular part of his ground, along the course of a brook, which runs also through a narrow neck of my father's property, by the intervention of which the count's territory was divided. This stripe of my father's ground would have been a purchase very convenient for Montauban; but, with that peculiar delicacy which our situation required, he never made the proposition of a purchase, but only requested that he might have leave to open a passage through an old wall, by which it was inclosed, that he might enjoy a continuation of that romantic path, which the banks of the rivulet afforded. His desire was expressed so politely, that it could not be refused. Montauban soon after paid a visit of thanks to my father, on the occasion: this last was pleased with an incident, which gave him back the power of conferring an obligation, and therefore, I presume, looked on his new acquaintance with a favourable eye; he praised his appearance to my mother and me; and since that day, they have improved their acquaintance into a very cordial intimacy.

In many respects, indeed, their sentiments are congenial. A high sense of honour is equally the portion of both. Montauban, from his long service in the army, and his long residence in Spain, carries it to a very romantic height. My father, from a sense of his situation, is now more jealous than ever of his. Montauban seems of a melancholy disposition. My father was far from being so once;

---

3. The absenteeism of the eighteenth-century aristocracy from their country estates was customary, and widely regarded as pernicious: Maria Edgeworth would focus on the issue in her Irish novels *Castle Rackrent* (1800) and *The Absentee* (1812), but it was also a notable preoccupation of late-eighteenth century Scots, for whom the departure of landowners for the Court in London was a source of anxiety.

but misfortune has now given his mind a tincture of sadness. Montauban thinks lightly of the world from principle. My father, from ill-usage, holds it in disgust. This last similarity of sentiment is a favourite topic of their discourse, and their friendship seems to increase from every mutual observation which they make. Perhaps it is from something amiss in our nature, but I have often observed the most strict of our attachments to proceed from an alliance of dislike.

There is something hard and unbending in the character of the count, which, though my father applauds it under the title of magnanimity, I own myself womanish enough not to like. There is an yielding weakness, which, to me, is more amiable than the inflexible right; it is an act of my reason to approve of the last; but my heart gives its suffrage to the first, without pausing to enquire for a cause. — I am awkward at defining; you know what I mean; the last is stern in Montauban, the first is smiling in Maria.

Mean time, I wish to feel the most perfect gratitude for his unwearied assiduity to oblige my father and his family. When I think on his uncommon friendship, I try to forget that severity which holds me somehow at a distance from him.

Though I meant a description, I have scrawled through most of my paper without beginning one. I have made but some slight sketches of his mind; of his person I have said nothing, which, from a woman to a woman, should have been mentioned the soonest. It is such as becomes a soldier, rather manly than handsome, with an air of dignity in his mien that borders on haughtiness. In short, were I to study for a sentence, I should say, that Montauban was made to command respect from all, to obtain praise from most, but to engage the affections of few.[4]

His company to-day was of importance to us. By ourselves

---

4. 'Sentence' is used here in the eighteenth-century sense of an aphorism or pithy saying; in his periodical, *The Rambler* (No. 79), Samuel Johnson describes 'a Greek writer of sentences [who] has laid down as a standing maxim, that he who believes not another on his oath, knows himself to be perjured'.

every one's look seemed the spy on another's. We were conscious of remembering what all affected to forget. Montauban's conversation reconciled us, without our being sensible of it.

My father, who (as it commonly happens to the aggressor in those cases) had perhaps felt more from his own harshness than either my mother or I, seemed happy to find an opportunity of being restored to his former familiarity. He was gayer, and more in spirits, than I have seen him for some time past. He insisted on the count's spending the evening with us. Montauban at first excused himself. He had told us, in the course of conversation, of his having appropriated the evening to business at home; but my father would listen to no apology, and the other was at last overcome. He seems, indeed, to feel an uncommon attachment to my father, and to enjoy more satisfaction in his company, than I should have expected him to find in the society of any one.

You are now, in the account of correspondence, I do not know how deep in my debt. I mean not to ask regular returns; but write to me, I entreat you, when you can; and write longer letters than your last. Put down every thing, so it be what you feel at the time; and tell every incident that can make me present with you, were it but the making up of a cap that pleases you. You see how much paper I contrive to blot with trifles.

Montauban to Segarva

You saw, my friend, with what reluctance I left Spain, though it was to return to the country of my birth, to the inheritance of my fathers. I trembled when I thought what a scene of confusion the strange mismanagement of my uncle had left me to disentangle; but it required only a certain degree of fortitude to begin that business, and it was much sooner concluded than I looked for. I have now almost wrought myself out of work, and yet the situation is not so disgusting as I imagined. I have long learned to despise that flippancy which characterizes my countrymen; yet, I know not how it is, they gain upon me in spite of myself; and while I resolve to censure, I am forced to smile.

From Paris, however, I fled, as if it had been infested with a pestilence. Great towns certainly contain many excellent persons; but vice and folly predominate so much, that a search after their opposites is beyond the limits of ordinary endurance; and, besides the superiority of numbers, the first are ever perked up to view, while the latter are solicitous to avoid observation.

In the country I found a different style of character. Here are impertinents who talk nonsense, and rogues who cheat where they can; but they are somewhat nearer nature in both. I met with some female relations, who stunned me with receipts in cookery, and prescriptions in physic; but they did not dictate to my taste in letters, or my judgment in philosophy. Ignorance I can bear without emotion, but the affectation of learning gives me a fit of the spleen.

I make indeed but an awkward figure among them; for I am forced, by representing my uncle, to see a number of our family friends, whom I never heard of. These good people, however, bear with me wonderfully, and I am not laughed at, as you predicted.

But they sometimes pester me with their civilities. It is their principle, that a man cannot be happy alone; and they tire me with their company, out of pure good nature. I have endeavoured to undeceive them: the greater part do not understand my hints; those who do, represent me as a sour ungracious being, whom Spain has taught pride and sullenness. This is well, and I hope the opinion will propagate itself apace. One must be somewhat hated, to be independent of folly.

There is but one of my neighbours, whose temper I find at all congenial to my own. He has been taught by misfortune to be serious: for that I love him; but misfortune has not taught him to be humble: for this I love him the more. There is a pride which becomes every man; a poor man, of all others, should possess it.

His name is Pierre de Roubigné. His family of that rank, which is perhaps always necessary to give a fixed liberality of sentiment. From the consequences of an unfortunate law-suit, his circumstances became so involved, that he was obliged to sell his paternal estate, and retire to a small purchase he had made in this province, which is situated in the midst of my territories here. My steward pointed it out to me, as a thing it was proper for me to be master of; and hinted, that its owner's circumstances were such as might induce him to part with it. Such is the language of those devourers of land, who wish to make a wilderness around them, provided they are lords of it. For my part, I find much less pleasure in being the master of acres, than the friend of men.

From the particulars of Mons. de Roubigné's story, which I learned soon after I came hither, I was extremely solicitous of his acquaintance: but I found it not easy to accomplish my desire; the distance which great minds preserve in adversity, keeping him secluded from the world. By humouring that delicacy, which ruled him in his acceptance of a new acquaintance, I have at last succeeded. He admits me as his guest, without the ceremony which the little folks around us oblige me to endure from them.

He does not think himself under the necessity of eternally talking to entertain me; and we sometimes spend a morning together, pleased with each other's society, though we do not utter a dozen sentences.

His youth has been enlightened by letters, and informed by travel; but what is still more valuable, his mind has been early impressed with the principles of manly virtue: he is liberal in sentiment, but rigid in the feelings of honour.

Were I to mark his failings, I might observe a degree of peevishness at mankind, which, though mankind may deserve, it is the truest independence not to allow them. He feels that chagrin at his situation, which constitutes the victory of misfortune over us — but I have not known misfortune, and am therefore not entitled to observe it.

His family consists of a wife and daughter, his only surviving child, who are equally estimable with himself. I have not, at present, time to describe them. I have given you this sketch of him, because I think he is such a man as might be the friend of my Segarva. There are so few in this trifling world, whose mutual excellence deserves mutual esteem, that the intervention of an hundred leagues should not bar their acquaintance: and we increase the sense of virtue in ourselves, by the consciousness of virtue in others.[5]

---

5. Montauban reveals himself here, like Henry Mackenzie, to be a follower of the 'moral sense' writings of the Scottish philosophers Francis Hutcheson (1694–1746) and Adam Smith (1723–1790), although his benevolence arises from a deep sense of duty rather than from natural impulse. Smith's *Theory of Moral Sentiments* (1759) is a pervasive influence on *Julia de Roubigné* (see note to p. 147 below).

Montauban to Segarva

I DESCRIBED to you, in my last, the father of that family, whose acquaintance I have chiefly cultivated since I came hither. His wife and daughter I promised to describe — at least such a promise was implied — perhaps I find pleasure in describing them — I have time enough at least for the description; — but no matter for the cause.

Madame de Roubigné has still the remains of a fine woman; and, if I may credit a picture in her husband's possession, was in her youth remarkably handsome. She has now a sort of stillness in her look, which seems the effect of resignation in adversity. Her countenance bears the marks of a sorrow, which we do not so much pity as revere; she has yielded to calamity, while her husband has struggled under its pressure, and hence has acquired a composure, which renders that uneasiness I remarked in him more observable by the contrast. I have been informed of one particular, which, besides the difference of sex, may, in a great measure, account for this. She brought Roubigné a very considerable fortune, the greatest part of which was spent in that unfortunate law-suit I mentioned. A consciousness of this makes the husband impatient under their present circumstances, from the very principle of generosity, which leads the wife to appear contented.

In her conversation, she is guided by the same evenness of temper. She talks of the world as of a scene where she is a spectator merely, in which there is something for virtue to praise, for charity to pardon; and smooths the spleen of her husband's observations by some palliative remark which experience has taught her.

One consolation she has ever at hand: *Religion*, the friend of calamity, she had cultivated in her most prosperous days. Affliction, however, has not driven her to enthusiasm;[6] her feelings of devotion are mild and secret, her expression gentle and charitable. I have always observed your outrageously religious, amidst their severity to their neighbours, manifest a discontent with themselves: spirits like Madame de Roubigné's have that inward peace which is easily satisfied with others. The rapturous blaze of devotion is more allied to vanity than to happiness: like the torch of the great, it distresses its owner, while it flames in the eye of the public; the other, like the rush-light of the cottager, cheers the little family within, while it seeks not to be seen of the world.

But her daughter, her lovely daughter! — with all the gentleness of her mother's disposition, she unites the warmth of her father's heart, and the strength of her father's understanding. Her eyes, in their silent state, (if I may use the term), give the beholder every idea of feminine softness; when sentiment or feeling animates them, how eloquent they are! When Roubigné talks, I hate vice, and despise folly; when his wife speaks, I pity both; but the music of Julia's tongue gives the throb of virtue to my heart, and lifts my soul to somewhat super-human.

I mention not the graces of her form; yet they are such as would attract the admiration of those, by whom the beauties of her mind might not be understood. In one as well as the other, there is a remarkable conjunction of tenderness with dignity; but her beauty is of that sort, on which we cannot properly decide independently of the soul, because the first is never uninformed by the latter.

To the flippancy, which we are apt to ascribe to females of her age, she seems utterly a stranger. Her disposition appears to lean, in an uncommon degree, towards the serious. Yet she breaks forth at times into filial attempts at gaiety, to amuse that disquiet which

---

6. In the eighteenth century, 'enthusiasm' referred to ill-regulated, extravagant or misdirected religious fervour.

she observes in her father; but even then it looks like a conquest over the natural pensiveness of her mind. This melancholy might be held a fault in Julia; but the fortune of her family has been such, that none but those who are totally exempted from thinking, could have looked on it with indifference.

It is only, indeed, when she would confer happiness on others, that she seems perfectly to enjoy it. The rustics around us talk of her affability and good humour with the liveliest gratitude; and I have been witness to several scenes, where she dispensed mirth and gaiety to some poor families in our neighbourhood, with a countenance as cheerful as the most unthinking of them all. At those seasons I have been tempted from the gravity natural to me, and borrowed from trifles a temporary happiness. Had you seen me yesterday dancing in the midst of a band of grape-gatherers, you would have blushed for your friend; but I danced with Julia.

I am called from my description by the approach of her whom I would describe. Her father has sent his servant to inform me, that his wife and daughter have agreed to accompany him in a walk as far as to a farm of mine, where I have set about trying some experiments in agriculture. Roubigné is skilful in those things: as for me, I know I shall lose money by them; but it will not be lost to the public; and if I can even show what will not succeed, I shall do something for the good of my neighbours. Methinks too, if Julia de Roubigné would promise to come and look at them — But I see their family from my window. Farewell.

LETTER VI.

Julia to Maria

You RALLY me on the subject of the Count de Montauban, with that vivacity I have so often envied you the possession of. You say, you are sure you should like him vastly. "What a blessing, in a remote province, where one is in danger of dying of ennui, to have this stiff, crusty, honourable Spaniard, to teaze and make a fool of!" I have no thoughts of such amusement, and therefore I do not like him vastly; but I confess, I begin to like him better than I did. He has lost much of that sternness, (dignity, my father calls it,) which used to chill me when I approached him. He can talk of common things in a common way; and but yesterday, he danced with me on the green amidst a troop of honest rustics, whom I wished to make happy at the small expense of sharing their happiness. All this, I allow, at first seemed foreign to the man; but he did not, as I have seen some of your wise people do, take great credit for letting himself down so low. He did it with a design of frankness, though some of his native loftiness remained in the execution.

We are much in his debt on the score of domestic happiness. He has become so far one of the family as to be welcome at all times, a privilege he makes very frequent use of; and we find ourselves so much at ease with him, that we never think even of talking more than we chuse, to entertain him. He will sit for an hour at the table where I am working, with no other amusement than that of twisting shreds of my catgut into whimsical figures.[7]

---

7. 'Catgut' was a coarse cloth material made from thick cord with a wide weave and used in embroidery or needlework.

I think that he also is not the worse for our society; I suppose him the happier for it, from the change in his sentiments of others. He often disputes with my father, and will not allow the world to be altogether so bad as he used to do. My father, who can now be merry at times, jokes him on his apostasy. He appealed to me this morning for the truth of his argument. I told him, I was unable to judge, because I knew nothing of the world. "And yet, (replied he gallantly,) it is from you one should learn to think better of it: I never knew, till I came hither, that it contained any thing so valuable as Mademoiselle de Roubigné." I think, he looked foolish when he paid me this compliment. I curtsied with composure enough. It is not from men like Montauban that one blushes at a compliment.

Besides the general addition to our good humour, his society is particularly useful to me. His discourse frequently turns on subjects, from the discussion of which, though I am somewhat afraid to engage in it, I always find myself the wiser. Amidst the toils of his military life, Montauban has contrived to find leisure for the pursuit of very extensive and useful knowledge. This, though little solicitous to display, he is always ready to communicate; and, as he finds me willing to be instructed, he seems to find a pleasure in instructing me.

My mother takes every opportunity of encouraging this sort of conversation. You have often heard her sentiments on the mutual advantage of such intercourse between the sexes. You will remember her frequent mention of a male friend, who died soon after her marriage, from whom, she has told us, she derived most of the little accomplishment her mind can boast of. "Men, (she used to say,) though they talk much of their friends, are seldom blest with a friend. The nature of that companionship, which they mistake for friendship, is really destructive of its existence; because the delicacy of the last shrinks from the rude touch of the former; and that, however pure in their own sentiments, the society which they see each other hold with third persons, is too gross not to break those tender links, which are absolutely essential to friendship. Girls, (she said,) easily form a connection of a more refined sort; but as it commonly begins with romance, it seldom outlasts the years of childhood, except when it degenerates into cabal and intrigue; but that the friendship of one of each sex, when so circumstanced as to be distant from love, (which she affirmed might be the case,) has that combination of strength and delicacy which is equally formed to improve and delight."

There may be much reason in her arguments; but I cannot, notwithstanding my esteem for him, easily think of Montauban as my friend. He has not yet quite obliterated the fears I felt on our first acquaintance. He has, however, done much to conquer them; and, if he goes on as he has begun, I know not what in time he may arrive at. Mean time, I am contented with Maria; our friendship has at least endured beyond the period assigned by my mother. Shall it not always endure? I know the answer which your heart will make — mine throbs while I think of it.

Montauban to Segarva

YOU COMPLAIN of my silence. In truth I have nothing to say but to repeat, what is very unnecessary, my assurances of friendship to Segarva. My life is of a sort that produces nothing; I mean in recital. To myself it is not vacant: I can be employed in marking the growth of a shrub; but I cannot describe its progress, nor even tell why its progress pleases me.

If the word society is confined to our own species, I enjoy very little of it. I should except that of the family I gave you an account of some time ago. I fear I am too often with them; I frequently resolve to be busy at home; but I have scarce sat down to my table, when the picture of Roubigné's parlour presents itself, and I think that my business may wait till to-morrow.

I blush to tell you what a fool I am grown; or is it that I am nearer the truth than formerly? I begin to entertain doubts of my own dignity, and to think that man is not altogether formed for the sublime place I used to allot him. One can be very happy with much less trouble, than very wise: I have discovered this at Roubigné's. It is but conquering the name of trifles, which our pride would give things, and my hours at Roubigné's are as importantly filled up as any employment could make them.

After all, what is our boasted philosophy to ourselves, or others? Its consequence is often borrowed, more from the language it speaks, than the object it pursues, and its attainments valued, more from their difficulty than their usefulness. But life takes its complexion from inferior things; and providence has wisely placed its real blessings within the reach of moderate abilities. We look for a station beyond them; it is fit that we too should have our reward; and it is found in our vanity. It is only from this cause that I sometimes blush, as if I were unworthily employed, when I feel myself happy in doing nothing at Mons. de Roubigné's fire-side.

Yet do not suppose that we are always employed in talking of trifles. She has a mind no less capable of important research, of exalted sentiment —

I am hastily called away; — it saves you the continuation of a very dull letter. I send this, such as it is, more as a title to receive one from you, than that it should stand for any thing of itself. Farewell.

Julia to Maria

PITY ME, Maria, pity me! even that quiet that my letters of late described which I was contented to call happiness, is denied me. There is a fatality which everywhere attends the family of the unfortunate Roubigné; here, to the abodes of peace, perplexity pursues it; and it is destined to find new distress, from those scanty sources to which it looked for comfort.

The Count de Montauban — why did he see me? why did he visit here? why did I listen to his discourse? though, heaven knows, I meant not to deceive him! — He has declared himself the lover of your Julia! — I own his virtues, I esteem his character, I know the gratitude too we owe him: from all these circumstances, I am doubly distressed at my situation; but it is impossible, it is impossible that I should love him. How could he imagine that I should? or how does he still continue to imagine, that I may be won to love him? I softened my refusal, because I would distress no man; Montauban of all men the least: but surely it was determined enough to cut off all hopes of my ever altering my resolution.

Should not his pride teach him to cease such mortifying solicitations? How has it, in this instance alone, forsaken him? Methinks, too, he has acted ungenerously in letting my mother know of his addresses. When I hinted this, he fell at my feet, and intreated me to forgive a passion so earnest as his, for calling in every possible assistance. Cruel! that, in this tenderest concern, that sex, which is naturally feeble, should have other weaknesses to combat besides its own.

I know my mother's gentleness too well to have much to fear

from her; but the idea of my father's displeasure is terrible. This morning when I intreated my mother not to mention this matter to him, she informed me of her having already told him. It was an affair, she said, of so much importance to his family, that she durst not venture to conceal it. There was something in the coolness of her words that hurt me; but I stifled the answer which I was about to make, and only observed, that of that family I was the nearest concerned. "You shall judge for yourself, my dear girl," said she, resuming the natural gentleness of her manner; "I will never pretend to control your affections. Your opinions I always hold it my duty to guide; experience, dearly bought perhaps, has given me some title to guide them. Believe me, there are dreams of romantic affection, which are apt to possess young minds, the reality of which is not to be found in nature. I do not blame you for doubting this at present; but the time will come when you will be convinced of its truth."

Is it so, Maria? Shall that period ever arrive, when my present feelings shall be forgotten? But, if it should, are they not *now* my conscience, and should I not be unjust to Montauban and myself, were I *now* to act against them?

═══

I have seen my father. He came into my room, in his usual way, and asked me, if I chose to walk with him. His words were the same they were wont to be; but I could discover, that his thoughts were different. He looked on me with a determined countenance, as if he prepared himself for contradiction. I concealed my uneasiness, however, and attended him with that appearance of cheerfulness, which I make it a point of duty to wear in his presence. He seemed to have expected something different; for I saw he was softened from that hostility, may I call it, of aspect, which he had assumed at first, and, during our walk, he expressed himself to me with unusual tenderness. Alas! too much so, Maria! Why am I obliged to offend him? When he called me the support and solace of his age, when he blessed Heaven, for leaving him, in the worst of his misfortunes, his Julia to comfort him — why could I not then, amidst my filial tears, when my heart should have poured itself out in duty and gratitude, why could I not then assure him of its obedience?

Write to me, for pity's sake, write to me speedily. — Assist me, counsel me, guide me — but say not that I should listen to Montauban.

Montauban to Segarva

I sit down to write to Segarva, with the idea of his presence at the time, and the idea was wont to be a pleasant one; it is now mixed with a sort of uneasiness, like that which a man feels, who has offended, and would ask to be forgiven. The consciousness of what I mean by this letter to reveal, hangs like guilt upon my mind; therefore it is that I have so long delayed writing. If you shall think it weakness — Yet I know not how I can bear chiding on this point.

But why should I doubt of your approving it? Our conversations on the sex might be just, but they touch not Julia de Roubigné. Could my friend but see, but know her, I should need no other advocate to excuse the change of my sentiments.

Let me tell him, then, of my passion for that loveliest of women; that it has prompted me to offer her a hand, which he has sometimes heard me declare should never give away my freedom. This sounded like something manly; but it was, in truth, a littleness of soul. He, who pauses in the exercise of every better affection of the heart, till he calculates the chances of danger or of ridicule, is the veriest of cowards; but the resolution, though frequently made, is seldom or never adhered to: the voice of nature, of wisdom, and of virtue, is against it.

To acquire such a friend as Julia de Roubigné — but friend is a word insignificant of the connection — to have one soul, one fate with her; to participate her happiness, to share her griefs! to be that single being to whom, the next to the Divinity, she pours out the feelings of her heart; to whom she speaks the gentlest of her wishes; to whom she sighs the most delicate of her fears! to grant those wishes, to soothe those fears! to have such a woman (like our guardian angel, without his superiority,) to whom we may unbosom our own! — the creation of pleasures is little; this is a creation of soul to enjoy them!

Call not mine the language of doating love; I am confident how much reason is on my side, and will now hear Segarva with patience.

He will tell me of that fascinating power which women possess when they would win us, which fades at once from the character of wife. — But I know Julia de Roubigné well; she has grown up under the eye of the best of parents, unschooled in the practices of her sex; she is ignorant of those arts of delusion, which are taught by the society of women of the world. I have had opportunities of seeing her at all seasons, and in every attitude of mind. — Her soul is too gentle for the touch of art; an effort of deceit would wring it even to torture.

He will remind me of the disparity of age, and tell me of the danger of her affections wandering from one, whom, on comparison with herself, she will learn to think an old man. — But Julia is of an order of beings superior to those, whom external form, and the trifling language of gallantry, can attract. — Had she the flippancy of mind which those shallow qualities are able to allure, I think, Segarva, she were beneath the election of Montauban.

I remember our former conversations on the subject of marriage, when we were both of one side; and that then you observed in me a certain wakeful jealousy of honour, which, you said, the smile of a wife on another man would rouse into disquiet. — Perhaps I have been sometimes too hasty that way, in the sense of affronts from men; but the nicety of a soldier's character, which must ever be out of the reach of question, may excuse it. I think I never shewed suspicion of my friends; and why to this lovely one, the delicacy of whose virtue I would vouch against the world, should I be more unjust than to others? — There is no fiend so malicious as to breathe detraction against my Julia.

In short, I have canvassed all your objections, and, I think, I have answered them all. Forgive me for supposing you to make them; and forgive me, when I tell you that, while I did so, methought I loved you less than I was wont to do.

But I am anticipating blessings which may never arrive; for the gentlest of her sex is yet cruel to Montauban. But, I trust, it is only the maiden coyness of a mind naturally fearful. She owned her esteem, her friendship: these are poor to the returns I ask; but they must be exchanged for sentiments more tender, they must yield to the ardour of mine. They must, they shall: I feel my heart expand with a glad foreboding, that tells it of happiness to come. While I enjoy it, I wish for something more: let me hear then that my Segerva enjoys it too.

Julia to Maria

YOU KNOW not the heart of your Julia; yet impute it not to a want of confidence in your friendship. Its perplexity is of a nature so delicate, that I am sometimes afraid even to think on it myself; and often, when I meant to reveal it to you, my utterance failed in the attempt.

The character you have heard of the Count de Montauban is just; it is perhaps even less than he merits: for his virtues are of that unbending kind, that does not easily stoop to the opinion of the world; to which the world, therefore, is not profuse of its eulogium. I revere his virtues, I esteem his good qualities; — but I cannot love him. — This must be my answer to others: But Maria has a right to something more; she may be told my weakness, for her friendship can pity and support it.

Learn then, that I have not a heart to bestow. — I blush even while I write this confession. — Yet to love merit like Savillon's cannot be criminal. — Why then do I blush again, when I think of revealing it?

You have seen him at Belville; alas! you know not his worth; it is not easy to know it. Gentle, modest, retired from notice, — it was the lot of your Julia to discover it. She prized it the more, that it was not common to all; and while she looked on it as the child of her own observation, it was vanity to know, it was virtue to cherish. — Alas! she was unconscious of that period, when it ceased to be virtue, and grew into passion.

But whither am I wandering? I meant only to relate; but our feelings speak for themselves, before we can tell why we feel.

Savillon's father and mine were friends; his father was

unfortunate, and mine was the friend of his misfortune; hence arose a sort of dependence on the one side, which on the other, I fear, was never entirely forgotten. I have sometimes observed this weakness in my father; but the pride that leads to virtue may be pardoned. He thinks of a man as his inferior, only that he may do him a kindness more freely. Savillon's family, indeed, was not so noble as his mind; my father warmly acknowledged the excellence of the last; but he had been taught, from earliest infancy, to consider a misfortune the want of the former.

After the death of old Savillon, my father's friendship and protection were transferred to his son; the time he could spare from study was commonly spent at Belville. He appeared to feel in his situation that dependence I mentioned; in mean souls, this produces servility; in liberal minds, it is the nurse of honourable pride. There was a silent melancholy about Savillon, which disdained the notice of superficial observers, and was never satisfied with superficial acquirement. His endowments did not attract the eye of the world; but they fixed the esteem and admiration of his friends. His friends indeed were few; and he seemed not to wish them many.

To know such a man; to see his merit; to regret that yoke which fortune had laid upon him — I am bewildered in sentiment again. — In truth, my story is the story of sentiment. I would tell you how I began to love Savillon; but the trifles, by which I now mark the progress of this attachment, are too little for description.

We were frequently together, at that time of life when a boy and girl are not alarmed at being together. Savillon's superior attainments made him a sort of master for your Julia. He used to teach me ideas; sometimes he flattered me, by saying, that, in his turn, he learned from me. Our feelings were often equally disgusted with many of the common notions of mankind, and we early began to form a league against them. We began with an alliance of argument; but the heart was always appealed to in the last resort.

The time at last came, when I began to fear something improper in our friendship; but the fears that should guard, betray us. They make pictures to our fancy, which the reason they call to their assistance cannot overcome. In my rambles through the woods at Belville, I have often turned into a different walk from that I first designed to take, because I suspected Savillon was there! — Alas! Maria, an ideal Savillon attended me, more dangerous than the real.

But it was only from his absence I acquired a certain knowledge of myself. I remember, on the eve of his departure, we were walking in the garden; my father was with us. He had been commending some carnation seeds, which he had just received from an eminent florist at Versailles. Savillon was examining some of them, which my father had put into his hand; and soon after, when we came to a small plot, which I used to call my garden, he sowed a few of them in a particular corner of it. I took little notice at the time; but, not long after he was gone, the flowers began to appear. You cannot easily imagine the effect this trifling circumstance had upon me. I used to visit the spot by stealth, for a certain conscious feeling prevented me going openly thither, and watched the growth of those carnations with the care of a parent for a darling child; and when they began to droop, (I blush, Maria, to tell it,) I have often watered them with my tears.

Such is the account of my own feelings; but who shall tell me those of Savillon? I have seen him look such things! — but, alas! Maria, our wishes are traitors, and give us false intelligence. His soul is too noble to pour itself out in those trivial speeches which the other sex often addresses to ours. Savillon knows not the language of compliment; yet methinks from Savillon it would please. May not a sense of his humble fortune prevent him from speaking what he feels? When we were first acquainted, Julia de Roubigné was a name of some consequence; fallen as she now is, it is now her time to be haughty, and Savillon is too generous to think otherwise. In our most exalted estate, my friend, we are not so difficult to win, as we are sometimes imagined to be: it unfortunately happens, that the best men think us the most so.

I know I am partial to my own cause; yet I am sensible of all the impropriety with which my conduct is attended. My *conduct*, did I call it? It is not my *conduct*, I err but in *thought*. Yet, I fear, I suffered these thoughts at first without alarm. They have grown up, unchecked, in my bosom, and now I would control them in vain. Should I know myself indifferent to Savillon, would not my pride set me free? I sigh, and dare not say that it would.

But there is something tenderer and less tumultuous in that feeling with which I now remember him, than when his presence use to alarm me. Obliged to leave France, where fortune had denied him an inheritance, he is gone to Martinique, on the invitation of an uncle, who has been several years settled in that island.[8] When I think of the track of ocean which separates us, my head grows dizzy as I think! — that this little heart should have its interests extended so far! that on the other side of the Atlantic, there should exist a being, for whom it swells with imaginary hope, and trembles, alas! much oftener trembles, with imaginary fear!

In such a situation, wonder not at my coldness to Montauban. I know not how it is; but, methinks, I esteem him less than I did, from the preposterous reason, that he loves me when I would not have him. I owe him gratitude in return, though I cannot give him love; but I involuntarily refuse him the first, because he asks the latter, which I have not to bestow.

Would that he had never seen your Julia! I expect not a life of happiness, but had looked for one of quiet. There is something in the idea even of peaceful sadness, which I could bear without repining; but I am not made for struggling with perplexity.

---

8. Martinique was a French slaveholding colony in the Caribbean, whose major crop was sugar cane. Slavery was not abolished there until 1848.

Julia to Maria

FROM YOUR letters, Maria, I always find comfort and satisfaction; and never did one arrive more seasonably than the last. When the soul is torn by contrary emotions, it is then that we wish for a friend to reconcile us to ourselves: such a friend am I blessed with in you. Advice from my Maria is the language of wisdom without its severity; she can feel what is due to nature, while she speaks what is required of prudence.

I have ever thought as you do, 'that it is not enough for a woman not to swerve from the duty of a wife; that to love another more than a husband, is an adultery of the heart; and not to love a husband with undivided affection, is a virtual breach of the vow that unites us.'

But I dare not own to my father the attachment from which these arguments are drawn. There is a sternness in his idea of honour, from which I shrink with affright. Images of vengeance and destruction paint themselves to my mind, when I think of his discovering that weakness which I cannot hide from myself. Even before my mother, as his wife, I tremble, and dare not disclose it.

How hard is the fate of your Julia! Unhappy from feelings which she cherished as harmless, yet denied even the comfort of revealing, except to Maria, the cause of her distress! Amidst the wreck of our family's fortunes, I shared the common calamity; must I now be robbed of the little treasure I had saved, spoiled of my peace of mind, and forbid the native freedom of my affections?

I am called to dinner. One of our neighbours is below, a distant relation of Montauban, with his wife and daughter. Another stranger, Lisette says, is also there, a captain of a ship, she thinks, whom she remembers having seen formerly at Belville. — Must I go then, and look unmeaning cheerfulness, and talk indifferent things, while my heart is torn with secret agitation? To feel distress, is painful; but to dissemble it, is torture.

I have now time to think, and power to express my thoughts. — It is midnight, and the world is hushed around me! After the agitation of this day, I feel something silently sad in my heart, that can pour itself out to my friend.

Savillon! cruel Savillon! — but I complain as if it were false-hood to have forgotten her, whom perhaps he never loved.

She too must forget him — Maria! he is the husband of another! That sea-captain, who dined with my father to-day, is just returned from Martinique. With a beating heart, I heard him questioned of Savillon. — With a beating heart, I heard him tell of the riches he is said to have acquired by the death of that relation with whom he lived; but judge of its sensations, when he added, that Savillon was only prevented, by that event, from marrying the daughter of a rich planter, who had been destined for his wife on the very day his uncle died, and whom he was still to marry as soon as decency would permit. 'And before this time,' said the stranger, 'he must be her husband.'

Before this time! — While I was cherishing romantic hopes; or, at least, while, amidst my distress, I had preserved inviolate the idea of his faith and my own. — But whither does this delusion carry me? Savillon has broken no faith; to me he never pledged it. Hide me, my friend, from the consciousness of my folly, or let it speak till its expiation be made, till I have banished Savillon from my mind.

Must I then banish him from my mind? Must I forget the scenes of our early days, the opinions we formed, the authors we read, the music we played together? There was a time when I was wont to retire from the profanity of vulgar souls to indulge the remembrance!

I heard somebody tap at my door. I was in that state of mind which every thing terrifies; I fancy I looked terrified, for my mother, when she entered, begged me, in a low voice, not to be alarmed.

"I come to see you, Julia," said she, "before I go to bed. Methought you looked ill at supper." — "Did I, mamma?" said I, "I am well enough; indeed I am." — She pressed my hand gently; I attempted to smile; it was with difficulty I forebore weeping.

"Your mind, child," continued my mother, "is too tender, I fear it is, for this bad world. You must learn to conquer some of its feelings, if you would be just to yourself; but I can pardon you, for I know how bewitching they are; but trust me, my love, they must not be indulged too far; they poison the quiet of our lives. Alas! we have too little at best! I am aware how ungracious the doctrine is; but it is not the less true. If you ever have a child like yourself, you will tell her this, in your turn, and she will not believe you."

I was now weeping outright; it was the only answer I could make. My mother embraced me tenderly, and begged me to be calm, and endeavour to rest. I gave her my promise to go soon to bed: I am about to perform it; but to rest, Maria! — Farewell.

LETTER XII.

Julia to Maria

WHILE I write, my paper is blotted by my tears. They fall not now for myself, but for my father; you know not how he has wrung my heart.

He had another appointment this day with that procureur, who once visited our village before.[9] — Sure, there is something terrible in that man's business. Alas! I formerly complained of my father's ill-humour, when he returned to us from a meeting with him; I knew not, unjust that I was, what reason he then might have for his chagrin; I am still ignorant of their transactions, but have too good ground for making frightful conjectures.

On his return in the evening, he found my mother and me in separate apartments. She has complained of a slight disorder, from cold, I believe, these two or three days past, and had lain down on a couch in her own room, till my father should return. I was left alone, and sat down to read my favourite Racine.

"Iphigenia!" said my father, taking up the book, "Iphigenia!"[10] He looked on me piteously as he repeated the word. I cannot make you understand how much that single name

---

9. Attorney or legal agent; prosecutor. Mackenzie draws on similarities between the French and Scottish legal systems here: the procureur or procurator was a feature only of ecclesiastical law in England.

10. In Euripides' Greek play, Iphigenia is sacrificed by her father Agamemnon in order to gain favourable winds for the Greek fleet on its way to Troy. In the French tragedy freely drawn from Euripides by Jean Racine (1679), Iphigénie obediently awaits her fate in deference to her father.

expressed, or how much that look. He pressed me to his bosom, and as he kissed me, I felt a tear on his cheek.

"Your mother is in her own chamber, my love." I offered to go and fetch her; he held my hand fast, as if he would not have me leave him. We stood for some moments thus, till my mother, who had heard his voice, entered the room.

We sat down by the fire, with my father between us. He looked on us alternately with an affected cheerfulness, and spoke of indifferent things in a tone of gaiety rather unusual to him; but it was easy to see how foreign those appearances were to the real movements of his soul.

There was at last a pause of silence, which gave them time to overcome him. We saw a tear, which he was unable to repress, begin to steal from his eye. "My dearest life!" said my mother, laying hold of his hand, and kissing it: I pressed the other in mine. "Yes," said he, "I am still rich in blessings, while these are left me. You, my love, have ever shared my fortune unrepining: I look up to you as to a superior Being, who, for all his benefits, accepts of our gratitude as the only recompense we have to make. This — this last retreat, where I looked for peace at least, though it was joined to poverty, we may soon be forced to leave! — Wilt thou still pardon, still comfort the man, whose evil destiny has drawn thee along with it to ruin? — And thou too, my child, my Julia! thou wilt not forsake thy father's grey hairs! Misfortune pursues him to the last: Do thou but smile, my cherub, and he can bear it still." I threw my head on his knees, and bathed them with my tears. "Do not unman me," he cried. "I would support my situation as becomes a man. — Methinks, for my own part, I could endure any thing — but my wife! my child! can they bear want and wretchedness!" — "They can bear any thing with you," said my mother. I started up, I know not how; I said something, I know not what; but, at that moment, I felt my heart roused as with the sound of a trumpet. My mother stood on one side, looked gently upwards, her hands, which were clasped together, leaning on my father's shoulder. He had one hand in his side, the other pressed on his bosom, his figure seeming to rise above itself, and his eye bent steadily forward. — Methought, as I looked on them, I was above the fears of humanity.

Le Blanc entered. "'Tis enough," said my father, taking one or two strides through the room, his countenance still preserving an air of haughtiness. "Go to my chamber," said he to Le Blanc, "I have some business for you." When they left the room, I felt the weakness of my soul return. I looked on my mother; she turned from me to hide her tears. I fell on her neck, and gave a loose to mine: "Do not weep, Julia!" was all she could utter, and she wept while she uttered it.

When Le Blanc returned, he was pale as ashes, and his hand shook so, that he could hardly carry in supper. My father came in a few minutes after him: he took his place at table as he was wont to do. — During the time of supper, I observed Le Blanc fix his eye upon him; and, when he answered some little questions put to him by my father, his voice trembled in his throat.

After being left by ourselves, we were for some time silent. My mother at last spoke through her tears: "Do not, my dearest Roubigné," said she, "add to our misfortunes by an unkind concealment of them. — Has any new calamity befallen us? — When we retired hither, did we not know the worst?" — "I am afraid not," answered he calmly, "but my fears may not be altogether just. Do not be alarmed, my love, things may turn out better than they appear. I was affected too much before supper, and could not conceal it. There are weak moments, when we are not masters of ourselves. When I looked on my Julia and you, when I thought on those treasures, I was a very coward; but I have resumed my fortitude, and I think I can await the decision calmly. You shall know the whole, my love; but let me prevail on you to be comforted in the mean time; let not our distresses reach us before their time." He rung for Le Blanc, and gave him directions about some ordinary matters for next day.

As I went up stairs to my room, I saw that poor fellow standing at the window in the stair-case. "What do you here," said I, "Le

Blanc?" — "Ah! Miss Julia," said he, "I know not well what I do." He followed me into my room, without my bidding him. "My master has spoken so to me! — When he called me out before supper, as you saw, I went with him into his closet: he wrote something down, as if he were summing up money. — 'Here are so much wages due to you, Le Blanc,' said he, putting the paper into my hand. 'You shall receive the money now; for I know not how long these louis may be mine to give you.' — I could not read the figures, I am sure I could not; I was struck blind, as it were, when he spoke so. He held out the gold to me: I drew back; for I would not have touched it for the world; but he insisted on my taking it, till I fell on my knees, and intreated him not to kill me by offering such a thing. At length he threw it down on his table, and I saw him wipe his eyes with his handkerchief. — 'My dear master!' said I, and I believe I took hold of his hand, for seeing him so, made me forget myself. — He waved his hand for me to leave the room; and, as I went down into the kitchen, if I had not burst into tears, I think I should have fainted away." —

What will our destiny do with us? But I have learned, of late, to look on misery with less emotion. My soul has sunk into a stupid indifference, and sometimes, when she is roused at all, I conceive a sort of pride in meeting distress with fortitude, since I cannot hope for the attainment of happiness. But my father, Maria! — thus to bear at once the weakness of age, the gripe of poverty, the buffets of a world with which his spirit is already at war! — there my heart bleeds again! The complaints I have made of those little harshnesses I have sometimes felt from him, rise up to my memory in the form of remorse. Had he been more perfectly indulgent, methinks I should have pitied him less.

———

I was alarmed by hearing my mother's bell. She had been seized with a sudden fit of sickness, and had almost fainted. She is now a good deal better, and endeavours to make light of it; but at this time I am weaker than usual, and every appearance of danger frightens me. She chid me for not having been a-bed. I leave this open till the morning, when I can inform you how she does.

—————

My mother has got up, though against the advice of my father and me. It may be fancy, but I think I see her eye languid and weighed down. I would stifle even the thoughts of danger, but cannot. Farewell.

Lisette to Maria

MADAM,

I AM commanded by my dear young lady to write to you, because she is not in a condition to write herself. I am sure I am little able either. I have a poor head for inditing at any time; and, at present, it is so full of the melancholy scenes I have seen, that it goes round, as it were, at the thoughts of telling them. When I think what a lady I have lost! — To be sure if ever there was a saint on earth, Madame de Roubigné was she — but heaven's will be done!

I believe Miss Julia wrote you a letter the day she was taken ill. She did not say much, for it was her way not to be troublesome with her complaints; but we all saw by her looks how distressed she was. That night my master lay in a separate apartment, and I sat up by her bed-side; I heard her tossing and restless all night long, and now and then when she got a few moments sleep, she would moan through it sadly, and presently wake with a start, as if something had frightened her. In the morning a physician was sent for, who caused her to be blooded; and we thought her the better for it: but that was only for a short time, and the next night she was worse than before, and complained of violent pains all over her body, and particularly her breast, and did not once shut her eyes to sleep. They took a greater quantity of blood from her now than at first, and in the evening she had a blister put on, and the doctor sat by her part of the night. All this time Miss Julia was scarce ever out of her mother's chamber, except some times for a quarter of an hour, when the doctor begged of her to go, and he and I were both attending my lady. My master, indeed, that last night took her away, and prevailed on her to put off her clothes, and go to bed; and I heard him say to her in a whisper, when they had got upon the stairs, "My Julia, have pity on yourself for my sake; and let me not lose both:" — And he wept, I saw, as he spoke; and she burst into tears.

The fourth day my lady continued much in the same way; but during the night she wandered a good deal, and spoke much of her husband and daughter, and frequently mentioned the Count de Montauban. The doctor ordered some things, I forget their proper name, to be laid to the soles of her feet, which seemed to relieve her head much; for she was more distinct towards morning, and knew me when I gave her drink, and called me by my name, which she had not done before, but had taken me for my young lady; but her voice was fainter than ever, and her physician looked more alarmed, when he visited her, than I had seen him do all the rest of her illness. My master was then in the room, and presently they went out together; my lady called me to her, and asked who had gone out; when I told her, she said, "I guess the reason; but, heaven be praised, I can think of it without terror."

Her daughter entered the room just then; she went up to her mother, and asked how she found herself? "More at ease, my child," said she, "but I will not deceive you into hope; I believe this momentary relief is a fatal symptom; my own feelings tell me so, and the doctor's looks confirm them." — "Do not speak so, my dearest mother! for heaven's sake, do not!" — was all she could answer.

The doctor returned along with my master. He felt my lady's pulse: Miss Julia looked up wildly in his face; my master turned aside his head; but my lady, sweet angel, was calm and gentle as a lamb. "Do not flatter me," said she, when the doctor let go her arm; "I know you think I cannot recover." — "I am not without hopes, madam," he replied, "though, I confess, my fears are stronger than my hopes." My lady looked upwards for a moment, as I have often seen her do in health. Her daughter flung herself on the bed; I thought she had fallen into a swoon, and wanted to lift her up in my arms, though I was all of a tremble, and could hardly support myself. She started up, and would have spoken to her mother; but she wept and sobbed, and could not. My lady begged her to be composed; my master could not speak, but he laid hold on her hand, and, with a sort of gentle force, led her out of the room.

My lady complained of a dryness in her mouth and lips: the doctor gave her a glass of water, into which he poured a little somewhat out of a phial; she thanked him when she had drunk it, and seemed to speak easier: he said he should leave her for a little. Monsieur de Roubigné came in; "Attend my daughter," said she to me; and I thought she wanted to be alone with my master.

I found Miss Julia in the parlour, leaning on the table, her cheek resting on her hand; when I spoke, she fell a-crying again. Soon after her father came in, and told her that her mother wished to see her: she returned along with my master, and they were some time together.

When I was called, I found my lady very low, by reason, as I suppose, she had worn herself out in speaking to them. The doctor said so too, when he returned; and in the afternoon, when I attended him down stairs, he said to me, "That excellent lady is going fast." He promised to see her again in two hours; but, before that time, we found she had grown much worse, and had lost her speech altogether; and when he came, he said nothing was to be done, but to make her as easy as possible, and offered to stay with her himself; which he did till about three next morning, when the dear good lady expired.

Her daughter fainted away, and it was a long time before the physician could recover her. It is wonderful how my master bears up, in order to comfort her; but one may see how heavy his grief is on him for all that. This morning, Miss Julia desired me to attend her to the chamber, where her mother's corpse is laid. I was surprised to hear her speak so calmly as she did; and, though I made so free as to dissuade her much at first, yet she persuaded me she could bear it well enough; and I went with her accordingly.

But when we came near the door, she stopped, and pulled me back into her room, and leaned on my arm, and fell into a violent fit of weeping; yet, when I begged her to give over thoughts of going, she said she was easy again, and would go. And thus two or three times she went and returned, till, at last, she opened the door in desperation, as one may say, and I went in close behind her. The first sight we saw was Monsieur de Roubigné at the bed-side, bending over the corpse, and holding one of its hands in his. "Support me, Lisette!" cried she; and leaned back on me again. My master turned about as she spoke: his daughter took courage, as it were, then, and walked up to the body, and took the hand that her father had just let drop, and kissed it. "My child!" said he. "My father!" answered my dear young lady; and they clasped one another in their arms. I could not help bursting into tears when I saw them; yet it was not altogether for grief neither; I know not how it was, but I weep when I think of it yet. May heaven bless them both, and preserve them to support one another!

My lady's bell rung, and she asked me if I had written to you? When I told her I had, she enquired if I had sent off the letter, and I was fain to say yes, lest she should ask me to read it, and I knew how bad it must be for her, to hear all I have told your ladyship repeated. I am sure it is a sad scrawl, and little worth your reading, were it not that it concerns so dear a friend of yours as my lady is; and I have told things just as they happened, and as they came up to my mind, which is indeed but in a confused way still. But I ever am, madam, with respect,

Your faithful and obedient servant,

LISETTE.

53

Julia to Maria

AT LAST, my Maria, I am able to write. In the sad society of my afflicted father, I have found no restraint on my sorrows. We have indulged them to the full: their first turbulence is subsided, and the still quiet grief that now presses on my bosom, is such as my friend may participate.

"Your loss is common to thousands." Such is the hackneyed consolation of ordinary minds, unavailing even when it is true. But mine is not common; it is not merely to lose a mother, the best, the most indulgent of mothers! — Think, Maria, think of your Julia's situation; how helpless, how forlorn she is! — A father pursued by misfortune to the wane of life; but, alas! he looks to her for support! he has outlived the last of his friends, and those who should have been linked to him by the ties of blood, the same fatal disputes, which ruined his fortune, have shaken from his side. — Beyond him, — and he is old, and affliction blasts his age! — beyond him, Maria, and but for thee, — the world were desolate around me.

My mother! — you have seen, you have known her. Her gentle, but assured spirit, was the tutelary power to which we ever looked up for comfort and protection; to the last moment it enlightened herself, and guided us. The night before she died, she called me to her bed-side: "I feel, my child," said she, "as the greatest bitterness of parting, the thought of leaving you to affliction and distress. — I have but one consolation to receive or to bestow, a reliance on that merciful Being, who, in this hour, as in all the past, has not forsaken me! Next to that Being, you will shortly be the only remaining support of the unfortunate Roubigné. — I had, of late, looked on one measure as the means of procuring his age an additional stay; but I will not prescribe your conduct, or warp your heart. I know the purity of your sentiments, the warmth of your filial affection; to those and the guidance of heaven" — She had spoken thus far with difficulty; her voice now failed in the attempt. — My father came into the room: he sat down by me: she stretched out her hand, and joining ours, which were both laid on the bed, together, she clasped them with a feeble pressure, leaned backward, seemingly worn out with the exertion, and looked up to heaven, as if directing us thither for that assistance which her words had bequeathed us, — her last words! for after that she could scarcely speak to be heard, and only uttered some broken syllables, till she lost the power of utterance altogether.

These words cannot be forgotten; they press upon my mind with the sacredness of a parent's dying instructions: But that measure they suggested — is it not against the dictates of a still superior power? I feel the thoughts of it as of a crime. Should it be so, Maria; or do I mistake the whispers of inclination for the suggestions of conscience? Yet I think I have searched my bosom impartially, and its answer is uniform. Were it otherwise, should it ever be otherwise, what would not your Julia do to smooth the latter days of a father, on whose grey hairs distresses are multiplied!

Methinks, since this last blow, he is greatly changed. That haughtiness of spirit, which seemed to brave, but in reality was irritated by misfortune, has left him. He looks calmly upon things; they affect him more, but hurt him less; his tears fall oftener, but they are less terrible than the sullen gloom which used to darken his aspect. I can now mingle mine with his, free to affliction, without uneasiness or fear; and those offices of kindness, which once my piety exacted, are now the offering of my heart.

Montauban has behaved, on this occasion, as became his character. How perfect were it, but for that weakness which regards your Julia! He came to see my father the day after that on which my mother died. "I will not endeavour," said he, "to stop the current of your grief: that comfort which the world offers, at times like these, flows not from feeling, and cannot be addressed to it. Your sorrow is just. I come to give you leisure to indulge it. Employ me in those irksome offices, which distress us more than the tears they oblige us to dry; think nothing too mean to impose on me, that can any how relieve my friend."

And this friend his daughter is forced to deprive him of! Such at least is the common pride of the sex, that will not brook any other connection where one is rejected. I am assailed by motives on every hand; but my own feelings are still unconquered. Support them, my ever-faithful Maria, if they are just; if not — but they cannot be unjust.

The only friend of my own sex, whom I possessed besides thee, is now no more! We needed no additional tie; yet, methinks, in the grief of my heart, I lean upon yours with increasing affection. Thou too — I will not say pity — thou shalt love me more.

Julia to Maria

I HAVE this moment received your answer to my last. Ah! my friend, it answers not as I wished. Is this forwardness in me to hear, with pleasure, only the arguments on one side, when my conduct should be guided by those on both?

You say, "It is from the absence of Savillon, that the impression he had made on my heart has gained its present strength; that the contemplation of distant objects is always stronger than the sense of present ones; and that, were I to see him now, were I daily to behold him the husband of another, I should soon grow tranquil at the sight. That it is injustice to myself, and a want of that proper pride, which should be the constant attendant of our sex, to suffer this unhappy attachment to overcome my mind; and that, after looking calmly on the world, you cannot allow so much force to those impressions, as our youth was apt to suppose in them. That they are commonly vanquished by an effort to vanquish them; and that the sinking under their pressure is one of those diseases of the mind, which, like certain diseases of the body, the exercise of its better faculties will very soon remove."

There is reason in all this; but while you argue from reason, I must decide from my feelings. In every one's own case, there is a rule of judging, which is not the less powerful that one cannot express it. I insist not on the memory of Savillon; I can forget him; I think I can — time will be kind that way — it is fit I should forget him — he is happy, as the husband of another. — But should I wed any man, be his worth what it may, if I feel not that lively preference for him which waits not for reasoning to persuade its consent? The suggestions I have had of Montauban's unwearied love, his uncommon virtues, winning my affections in a state of wedlock, I have always held a very dangerous experiment; there is equivocation in those vows, which unite us to a husband, our affection for whom we leave to contingency. — "But I already esteem and admire him." — It is most true! — why is he not contented with my esteem and admiration? If those feelings are to be ripened into love, let him wait that period, when my hand may be his without a blush. This I have already told him; he almost owned the injustice of his request, but pleaded the ardour of passion in excuse. Is this fair dealing, Maria? that his feelings are to be an apology for his suit, while mine are not allowed to be a reason for refusal?

=====

I am called away by my father; I heard the count's voice below some time before. There was a solemnity in my father's manner of asking me down, which indicates something important in this visit. You shall hear what that is before this letter is closed. — Again! he is come to fetch me.

=====

Maria! let me recover my surprise! Yet why should I be surprised at the generosity of Montauban? I know the native nobleness of his soul. — Was it in such a girl as me to enfeeble it so long?

My father led me into the parlour. Montauban was standing in a pensive posture; he made me a silent bow. I was placed in a chair, standing near another which the count had occupied before: He sat down. My father walked to the window, his back was to us. Montauban put himself once or twice into the attitude of speaking: But we were still silent.

My father turned and approached us. "The count has something to communicate, Julia. — Would you choose, Sir, that it should be addressed to her alone?" "No," answered he, "it is an expiation to both, and both should hear it made. I fear I have, unwittingly, been the cause of disquiet to a family, whose society, for some time past, has been one of the chief sweeteners of my life. They know my gratitude for the blessing of that intimacy they were kind enough to allow me. When I wished for a more tender connection, they could not blame my wish; but, when I pressed it so far as to wound their peace, I was unworthy of the esteem they had formerly given, an esteem I cannot now bear to lose. When I cease my suit, Miss Julia, let it speak, not a diminution, but an increase of my affection. If that regard, which you often had the generosity to confess for me, was impaired by my addresses, let me recover it by this sacrifice of my hopes; and while I devote to your quiet the solicitations of my love, let it confirm to me every privilege of the most sacred friendship."

Such were the words of Montauban. I know not what answer I made: I remember a movement of admiration, and no more. At that instant, he seemed nobler than ever; and when, in spite of his firmness, a tear broke forth, my pity almost carried me beyond my esteem. How happy might this man make another! Julia de Roubigné is fated to be miserable!

* * * * * *

The Count de Montauban to Mons. Duvergne, at Paris

* * * * * * *

I have sent only three of the bills I proposed in my last to remit; that for five thousand, and the other for twelve thousand livres, at short dates, I have retained, as, I believe, I shall have use for them here. You may discount some of the others, if you want money for immediate use, which, however, I imagine, will not be the case.

I beg you may, immediately on receipt of this, send the inclosed letter as directed. The name in the superscription I have made Vervette, though my steward, from whom I take it, is not sure if it be exactly that; but, as he tells me the man is a procureur of some practice, and is certain as to the place of his residence, I imagine you will have no difficulty in finding him. I wish my letter to reach him in Paris; but if you hear that he is gone into the country, send me notice by the messenger, who is to fetch down my uncle's papers, by whom I shall receive your answer sooner than by post.

* * * * * * *

Lisette to Maria

MADAM,

I MAKE bold to write this, in great haste, because I am sensible of your friendship for my lady, and that you will thank me for giving you an opportunity of trying to serve her father and her in their present distress. She, poor lady, is in such a situation as not to be able to write; and besides, she is so noble-minded, that I dare be sworn she would not tell you the worst, least it should look like asking your assistance.

How shall I tell you, madam? My poor master is in danger of being forced away from us, and thrown into prison! a debt, it seems, owing to some people in Paris, on account of expences about that unfortunate law-suit, has been put into the hands of a procureur, who will not hear of any delay in the payment of it; and he was here this morning, and told my master, as Le Blanc overheard, that, if he could not procure the money in three hours time, he must attend him to a jail. My master wished to conceal this from his daughter, and desired the procureur to do his duty, without any noise or disturbance; but Le Blanc had scarcely gone up stairs when she called him, and enquired about that man's business; and he could not hide it, his heart was so full, and so he told her all that had passed below. Then she flew down to her father's room, and hung about him in such a manner, weeping and sobbing, that it would have melted the heart of a savage; and so, to be sure, I said to the procureur: but he did not mind me a bit, nor my lady neither, though she looked so as I never beheld her in all my life; and I was terrified to see her so, and said all I could to comfort her, but to no purpose. At last a servant of the procureur brought him a letter, and presently he went out of the house, but left two of his attendants to watch that my master should not escape; and they are now here, and they say that he cannot grant any respite; but that, as sure as can be, when he returns, he will take away Mons. de Roubigné to prison. I send this by a boy, a nephew of Le Blanc's, who serves a gentleman in this province, who is just now going to post to Paris, and the boy called on his way, by good fortune, to see his uncle. I am, in haste, your very faithful and obedient servant,

LISETTE.

My lady is much more composed now, and so is my master. The procureur has not returned yet, and I have a sort of hope; yet God knows whence it should be, except from your ladyship.

Lisette to Maria

To be sure, madam, you must have been much affected with the distress in our family, of which I informed you in my last, considering what a friendship there is between my dear lady and you. And now I am much vexed, that I should have given you so much uneasiness in vain, and send this to let you know of the happy deliverance my master has met with, from that most generous of men the Count de Montauban; I say, the most generous of men, as to be sure he is, to advance so large a sum without any near prospect of being repaid, and without ever being asked to do such a favour; for I verily believe my master would die before he would ask such a favour of any one, so high-minded he is, notwithstanding all his misfortunes. He is just now gone to see the count; for that noble-hearted gentleman would not come to our house, lest, as Monsieur de Roubigné said, he should seem to triumph in the effects of his own generosity. Indeed, the thing was done as if it had been done by witchcraft, without one of this family suspecting such a matter; and the procureur never came back at all, only sent a paper, discharging the debt, to one of the men he had left behind, who, upon that, behaved very civilly, and went away with much better manners, forsooth, than they came; but Le Blanc followed them to the village, where they met the procureur, and thus it was that we discovered the debt to have been paid by the count, who, it seems, had sent that letter, but without a name, which the procureur received, when he left us at the time I wrote your ladyship last.

———

Monsieur de Roubigné is returned from his visit to the Count de Montauban, and has been a long time closeted with my lady;

and, to be sure, something particular must have passed, but what it is I cannot guess; only I am certain it is something more than common, because I was in the way when they parted, and my lady passed me, and I saw by her looks that there had been something. When she went into her own chamber, I followed her, and there she sat down, leaning her arm on her dressing-table, and gave such a sigh as I thought her heart would have burst with it. Then I thought I might speak, and asked if she was not well? — "Very well, Lisette," said she; but she said it as if she was not well for all that, breathing strongly as she spoke the words, as one does when one has run one's self out of breath. "Leave me, child," said she; "I will call you again by and bye." And so I left her as she bid me; and as I went out of the room, shutting the door softly behind me, I heard her start up from her chair, and say to herself, "The lot is cast!" I think that was it.

—

My master has been all this while in his study writing, and just now he called Le Blanc, and gave him a letter for the Count de Montauban; and Le Blanc told me, as he passed, that Monsieur de Roubigné looked gayer, and more in spirits than usual, when he gave it him. My lady is still in her chamber alone, and has never called me, as she promised. Poor dear soul! I am sure I would do any thing to serve her, that I would; and well I may, for she is the kindest, sweetest lady to me, and so indeed she is to every body.

And now, madam, I am sure I should ask a thousand pardons for using the freedom to write to you in such a manner, just by starts, as things happen. But I am sensible your ladyship will not impute my doing so to any want of respect, but only to my desire of giving your ladyship an account of the situation of my lady, and of this family; which you were so condescending as to say, after my first letter, you were much obliged to me for giving you, and begged that it might be in my own style, which, to be sure, is none of the best; but which your ladyship will be so good as pardon, especially as I am, when I write to you about these things, in a flutter, as one may say, as well as having little time to order my expressions for the best. I am, honoured madam,

With due respect,
Your faithful
And obedient servant,

LISETTE.

LETTER XIX.

Julia to Maria

IN THE intricacies of my fate, or of my conduct, I have long been accustomed to consider you my support and my judge. For some days past these have come thick upon me; but I could not find composure enough to state them coolly even to myself. At this hour of midnight, I have summoned up a still recollection of the past; and with you, as my other conscience, I will unfold and examine it.

The ready zeal of my faithful Lisette has, I understand, saved me a recital of the distress in which my father found himself involved, from the consequences of that unfortunate law-suit we have so often lamented. I could only share it with him; but a more effectual friend stepped forth in the Count de Montauban. His generosity relieved my father, and gave him back to freedom and your Julia.

The manner of his doing this was such as the delicacy of a mind, jealous of its own honour, would prompt in the cause of another's. I thought I saw a circumstance, previous to the count's performing it, which added to that delicacy. My father did not then perceive this; it was not till he waited on Montauban, that the force of it struck his mind.

When he returned home, I saw some remains of that pride, which formerly rankled under the receipt of favours it was unable to return. "My Julia," said he, "your father is unhappy; every way unhappy; but it is fit I should be humble — Pierre de Roubigné must learn humility!" He uttered these words in a tone that frightened me; — I could not speak. He saw me confused, I believe; and putting on a milder aspect, took my hand and kissed

66

it. — "Heaven knows, that, for myself, I rate not life and liberty at much; — but, when I thought what my child must suffer — I alone am left to protect her — and I am old and weak, and must ask for that assistance which I am unable to repay." — "The generous, Sir," said I, "know from their own hearts what yours can feel: all beyond is accident alone." — "The generous, indeed, my child! but you know not all the generosity of Montauban. — When he tore himself from those hopes which his love had taught him; when he renounced his pretensions to that hand, which I know can alone confer happiness on his life; it was but for a more delicate opportunity of relieving thy father. — 'I could not,' said he, 'while I sought your daughter's love, bear the appearance of purchasing it by a favour; now, when I have renounced it for ever, I am free to the offices of friendship.' — Had you seen him, Julia, when he pronounced this *for ever*! great as his soul is, he wept! By Heaven, he wept, at pronouncing it! — These tears, Julia, these tears of my friend! — Would I had met my dungeon in silence; — they had not torn my heart thus!"

Maria, mine was swelled to a sort of enthusiastic madness — I fell at his feet. —

"No, my father, they shall not. — Amidst the fall of her family, your daughter shall not stand aloof in safety. She should have shared the prison of her father in the pride of adversity; behold her now the partner of his humiliation! Tell the Count de Montauban, that Julia de Roubigné offers that hand to his generosity, which she refused to his solicitation; — tell him also she is above deceit: she will not conceal the small value of the gift. 'Tis but the offering of a wretch, who would somehow requite the sufferings of her father, and the services of his friend. If he shall now reject it, that ugly debt, which his unhappiness lays us under, will be repaid in the debasement she endures; if he accepts of it as it is, tell him its mistress is not ignorant of the duty that should attend it."

My father seemed to recover at my words; yet surprise was mixed with the satisfaction his countenance expressed. "Are these your sentiments, my love?" pressing my hand closer in his. The heroism of duty was wasted — I answered him with my tears. "Speak, my Julia, coolly! and let not the distress of your father warp your resolution. He can endure any thing; even his gratitude shall be silenced." — My fortitude revived again. — "There is some weakness, Sir, attends even our best resolves: mine are not without it; but they are fixed, and I have spoken them." He asked if he might acquaint Monsieur de Montauban. "Immediately, Sir," I answered, "if you please; the sooner he knows my resolution, the more will he see it flowing from my heart." My father went into his study, and wrote a letter, which he read to me. It was not all I could have wished, yet I could not mend it by correction. Who shall give words to the soul at such a time? My very thoughts are not accurate expressions of what I feel: there is something busy about my heart, which I cannot reduce into thinking. — Oh! Maria!

Montauban came immediately on the receipt of this letter; we did not expect him that night; we were at supper. In what a situation was your Julia while it lasted! In this terrible interval, I was obliged to meet his eye sometimes, in addressing ordinary civilities to him. To see him, to speak to him thus, while the fate of my life was within the power of a few little words, was such torture, as it required the utmost of my resolution to bear. My father saw it, and put as speedy an end to our meal as possible. — We were left alone.

My father spoke first, not without hesitation. — Montauban was still more confused; but it was the confusion of a happy man. He spoke some half sentences about the delicacy of my sentiments and his own; but was entangled there, and I think not able to extricate himself. At last, turning fuller towards me, who sat the silent ~~victim~~ of the scene, (why should I score through that word when writing to you? yet it is a bad one, and I pray you to forgive it,) he said, he knew his own unworthiness of that hand, which my generosity had now allowed him to hope for; but that every endeavour of his future life — the rest was common place; for his sex have but one sort of expression for the exulting modesty of success. — My father put my hand in his — I was obliged to raise my eyes from the ground, and look on him; his were bent earnestly on me: there was too, too much joy in them, Maria; mine could not bear them long. — "That hand," said my father, "is the last treasure of Roubigné. Fallen as his fortunes are, not the wealth of worlds had purchased it: to your friendship, to your virtue, he is blessed in bequeathing it." — "I know its value," said the count, "and receive it as the dearest gift of heaven and you." — He kissed my hand with rapture. —

It is done, and I am Montauban's for ever! —

Montauban to Segarva

GIVE ME joy, Segarva, give me joy — the lovely Julia is mine. Let not the torpid considerations of prudence, which your last letter contained, rise up to check the happiness of your friend, or that which his good fortune will bestow on you. Trust me thy fears are groundless — didst thou but know her as I do! — Perhaps I am more tender that way than usual; but there were some of your fears I felt a blush in reading. Talk not of the looseness of marriage-vows in France, nor compare her with those women of it, whose heads are giddy with the follies of fashion, and whose hearts are debauched by the manners of its votaries. Her virtue was ever above the breath of suspicion, and I dare pledge my life, it will ever continue so. But that is not enough; I can feel as you do, that it is not enough. I know the nobleness of her soul, the delicacy of her sentiments. She would not give me her hand except from motives of regard and affection, were I master of millions. I rejoice that her own situation is such, as infers no suspicion of interestedness in me; were she not Julia de Roubigné, I would not have wedded her with the world for her dower.

You talk of her former reluctance; but I am not young enough to imagine, that it is impossible for a marriage to be happy without that glow of rapture, which lovers have felt, and poets described. Those starts of passion are not the basis for wedded felicity, which wisdom would chuse, because they are only the delirium of a month, which possession destroys, and disappointment follows. — I have perfect confidence in the affection of Julia, though it is not of that intemperate kind which some brides have shewn. Had you seen her eyes how they spoke, when her father gave me her hand! there was still reluctance in them, — a reluctance more winning than all the flush of consent could have made her. Modesty and fear, esteem and gratitude, darkened and enlightened them by turns; and those tears, those silent tears, which they shed, gave me a more sacred bond of her attachment, than it was in the power of words to have formed.

I have sometimes allowed myself to think, or rather I have supposed you thinking, it might be held an imputation on the purity of her affection, that from an act of generosity towards her father, (with the circumstances of which I was under the necessity of acquainting you in my last,) her hand became rather a debt of gratitude, than a gift of love. But there is a deception in those romantic sounds, which tell us, that pure affection should be unbiassed in its disposal of a lover or a mistress. If they say, that affection is a mere involuntary impulse, neither waiting the decisions of reason, nor the dissuasives of prudence, do they not in reality degrade us to machines, which are blindly actuated by some uncontrollable power? If they allow a woman reasonable motives for her attachment, what can be stronger than those sentiments which excite her esteem, and those proofs of them which produce her gratitude?

But why do I thus reason on my happiness? — I feel no fears, no suspicion of alloy to it; and I will not search for them in abstract opinion, or in distant conjecture.

Tuesday next is fixt for the day that is to unite us; the show and ceremony that mingle so ill with the feelings of a time like this, our situation here renders unnecessary. A few of those simple ornaments, in which my Julia meets the gaze of the admiring rustics around us, are more congenial to her beauty than all the trappings of vanity or magnificence. We propose passing a week or two here, before removing to Montauban, where I must then carry my wife, to show my people their mistress, and receive that sort of homage, which I hope I have taught them to pay from the heart. Those relations of my family, who live in that neighbour-hood, must come and learn to love me better than they did.

Methinks, I shall be more easily pleased with them than I formerly was. I know not if it is nobler to despise insignificant people, than to bear with them coolly; but I believe it is much less agreeable. The asperities of our own mind recoil on itself. Julia has shown me the bliss of losing them.

Could I hope for my Segarva at Montauban? — Much as I doat on my lovely bride, there wants the last approval of my soul, till he smiles on this marriage, and blesses it. I know, there needs only his coming thither to grant this. I anticipate your answer, that now it is impossible; but let it be a debt on the future, which *the first* of your leisure is to pay. Meantime believe me happy, and add to my happiness by telling me of your own.

LETTER XXI.

Julia to Maria

WHY SHOULD I tease you by writing of those little things which tease me in the doing? They tease, yet perhaps they are useful. At this time, I am afraid of a moment's leisure to be idle, and am even pleased with the happy impertinence of Lisette, whose joy, on my account, gives her tongue much freedom. I call her often, when I have little occasion for her service, merely that I may have her protection from solitude.

For the same reason I am somehow afraid of writing to you, which is only another sort of thinking. Do not therefore expect to hear from me again till after Tuesday at soonest. Maria! you remember our fancy at school of showing our friendship, by setting down remarkable days of one another's little joys and disappointments. Set down *Tuesday* next for your Julia — but leave its property blank. — Fate will fill it up one day!

Lisette to Maria

MADAM,

I HOPE my lady and you will both excuse my writing this, to give you notice of the happy event which has happened in our family. I made so bold as to ask her if she intended writing to you. "Lisette," said she, "I cannot write, I cannot indeed." So I have taken up the pen, who am a poor unworthy correspondent; but your ladyship's goodness has made allowances for me in that way before, and I hope will do so still.

The ceremony was performed yesterday. I think I never saw a more lovely figure than my lady's; she is a sweet angel at all times, but I wish your ladyship had seen how she looked then. She was dressed in a white muslin night-gown, with striped laylock[11] and white ribbands: her hair was kept in the loose way you used to make me dress it for her at Belville, with two waving curls down one side of her neck, and a braid of little pearls — you made her a present of them. And to be sure, with her dark-brown locks resting upon it, her bosom looked as pure white as the driven snow. — And then her eyes, when she gave her hand to the count! — they were cast half down, and you might see her eye-lashes, like strokes of a pencil, over the white of her skin — the modest gentleness, with a sort of sadness too, as it were, and a gentle heave of her bosom at the same time. — O! madam, you know I have not language, as my lady and you have, to describe such things; but it made me cry, in truth it did, for very joy and admiration. There was a tear in my master's eye too, though I believe two

---

11. 'Laylock': lilac.

happier hearts were not in France than his and the Count de Montauban's. I am sure, I pray for blessings on all three, with more earnestness, that I do, than for myself.

It seems, it is settled that the new married couple will not remain long here, but set out, in a week or two hence, for the count's principal seat, about six leagues distant from his house in our neighbourhood, which is not large enough for entertaining the friends, whose visits they must receive on this joyful occasion. I fancy Monsieur de Roubigné will be much with them, though I understand he did not chuse to accept of the count's pressing invitation to live with his daughter and him; but an elderly lady, a relation of my dear mistress that is gone, is to keep house for him.

I must break off now, for I hear my lady's bell ring, and your ladyship may believe we are all in a sort of buzz here. I dare to say she will not fail to write to you soon; but meantime, hoping you will accept of this poor scrawling letter of mine, I remain, with due respect,

Your most faithful
And obedient servant.

LISETTE.

P.S. My lady is to have me with her at the Chateau de Montauban; and to be sure, I am happy to attend her, as I could willingly spend all the days of my life with so kind a lady, and so good conditioned. The count likewise has been so good to me, as I can't tell how; and said, that he hoped my mistress and I would never part, "If she does not grow jealous," said he, merrily, "of so handsome a maid." — And at that we all laughed, as to be sure we might. My lady will be a happy lady, I am sure.

Julia to Maria

MY FRIEND will, by this time, be chiding me for want of attention to her; yet, in truth, she has seldom been absent from my thoughts. Were we together but for a single hour, I should have much to tell you; but there is an intricacy in my feelings on this change of situation, which, freely as I write to you, I cannot manage on paper. I can easily imagine what you would first desire to know, though perhaps it is the last question you would put. The *happiness* of your Julia, I know, is ever the warmest object of your wishes. — Ask me not, why I cannot answer even this directly. Be satisfied when I tell you, that I ought to be happy. — Montauban has every desire to make me so. —

One thing I wish to accomplish towards his peace and mine. The history of this poor heart I have entrusted only to your memory and my own: I will endeavour, though I know with how much difficulty, henceforth to forget it for ever. You must assist me, by holding it a blank, which recollection is no more to fill up. I know the weakness of my sex; myself of that sex the weakest: I will not run the risk of calling up ideas which were once familiar, and may not now be the less dangerous, nor the less readily listened to, for the pain they have caused. My husband has now a right to every better thought; it were unjust to embitter those hours which are but half the property of Julia de Montauban, with the remembrance of former ones, which belonged to sadness and Julia de Roubigné.

We are on the eve of our departure for the family-castle of Monsieur de Montauban. My father, whose happiness, at present, is a flattering testimony, as well as a support to my piety, accompanies us thither, but is soon to return home, where our cousin, La Pelliere, whom you may remember having seen with my mother in Paris, is to keep house for him. This separation I cannot help looking to as a calamity; yet, I believe his reasons for it are just. What a change in a woman's situation does this momentous connection make? — I will think no more of it. — Farewell.

━━

Yet a few words, to own my folly at least, if I cannot amend it. I went to assort some little articles of dress for carrying home with me; while I was rummaging out a drawer to find one of them, a little picture of Savillon, drawn for him when a boy, by a painter who was accidentally in our neighbourhood, crossed me in the way. You cannot easily imagine how this circumstance disconcerted me. I shut the drawer as if it had contained a viper; then opened it again; and again the countenance of Savillon, mild and thoughtful, (for even then it was thoughtful,) met my view! — Was it a consciousness of *guilt*, that turned my eye involuntarily to the door of the apartment? — Can there be any in accidentally thinking of Savillon? — Yet I fear I looked too long, and too impassionedly on this miniature. It was drawn with something sorrowful in the countenance, and methought it looked then more sorrowful than ever.

The question comes strong upon me, How I should like that my husband had seen this? In truth, Maria, I fear my keeping this picture is improper; yet at the time it was painted, there was one drawn for me by the same hand, and we exchanged resemblances without any idea of impropriety. Ye unfeeling decorums of the world! — Yet it is dangerous, is it not, my best monitor, to think thus? — Yet, were I to return the picture, would it not look like a suspicion of myself? — I will keep it till you convince me I should not.

Montauban and virtue! I am yours. Suffer but one sigh to that weakness which I have not yet been able to overcome. My heart, I trust, is innocent — blame it not for being unhappy.

Julia to Maria

MY FATHER was with me this morning, in my chamber, for more than an hour. We sat, sometimes silent, sometimes speaking interrupted sentences, and tears were frequently all the intercourse we held. Lisette coming in, to acquaint us that Montauban was in the parlour waiting us, at length put an end to our interview. "Julia," said my father, "I imagined I had much to say to you; but the importance of my thoughts, on your behalf, stifles my expression of them. There are moments when I cannot help looking to that separation, which your marriage will make between us, as if it were the loss of my child; yet I have fortitude enough to resist the impression, and to reflect, that she is going to be happy with the worthiest of men. My instruction for your conduct in that state you have just entered into, your own sentiments, I trust, would render unnecessary, were they in no other way supplied; but I discovered lately, in your mother's bureau, a paper, which still farther supersedes their necessity. It contains some advices, which experience and observation had enabled her to give, and her regard for you had prompted her to write down. 'Tis, however, only a fragment, which accident, or diffidence of herself, has prevented her completing; but it is worthy of your serious perusal, and you will read it with more warmth than if it came from a general instructor." He left the paper with me; I have read it with the care, with the affection it deserves; I send a copy of it now, as I would every good thing, for the participation of my friend. She cannot read it with the interest of a daughter; but she will find it no cold, no common lecture. It speaks, if I am not too partial to the best of mothers, the language of prudence, but not of artifice; it would mend the heart by sentiment, not cover it with dissimulation. She, for whose use it was written, has need of such a monitor, and would listen to no other; if she has paid any debt to prudence, it was not from the obligation of wisdom, but the impulse of feeling.

═══

For my daughter Julia

"BEFORE THIS can reach you, the hand that writes it, and the heart that dictates, will be mouldering in the grave. I mean it to supply the place of some cautions, which I should think it my duty to deliver to you, should I live to see you a wife. The precepts it contains, you have often heard me inculcate; but I know that general observations on a possible event, have much less force than those which apply to our immediate condition. In the fate of a woman, marriage is the most important crisis: it fixes her in a state beyond all others the most happy, or the most wretched; and though mere precept can perhaps do little in any case, yet there is a natural propensity to try its efficacy in all. She, who writes this paper, has been long a wife, and a mother: the experience of the one, and the anxiety of the other, prompt her instructions; and she has been too happy in both characters to have much doubt of their truth, or fear of their reception.

"Sweetness of temper, affection to a husband, and attention to his interests, constitute the duties of a wife, and form the basis of matrimonial felicity. These are indeed the texts from which every rule for attaining this felicity is drawn. The charms of beauty, and the brilliancy of wit, though they may captivate in the mistress, will not long delight in the wife: they will shorten even their own transitory reign, if, as I have seen in many wives, they shine more for the attraction of every body else than of their husbands. Let the pleasing of that one person be a thought never absent from your conduct. If he loves you as you would wish he should, he will bleed at heart should he suppose it for a moment withdrawn: if he does not, his pride will supply the place of love, and his resentment that of suffering.

"Never consider a trifle what may tend to please him. The great articles of duty he will set down as his own; but the lesser attentions he will mark as favours: and trust me, for I have experienced it, there is no feeling more delightful to one's self, than that of turning those little things to so precious a use.

"If you marry a man of a certain sort, such as the romance of young minds generally paints for a husband, you will deride the supposition of any possible decrease in the ardour of your affections. But wedlock, even in its happiest lot, is not exempted from the common fate of all sublunary blessings; there is ever a delusion in hope, which cannot abide with possession. The rapture of extravagant love will evaporate and waste; the conduct of the wife must substitute in its room other regards, as delicate, and more lasting. I say the conduct of the wife; for marriage, be a husband what he may, reverses the prerogative of sex; his will expect to be pleased, and ours must be sedulous to please.

"This privilege a good-natured man may wave: he will feel it, however, due; and third persons will have penetration enough to see, and may have malice enough to remark, the want of it in his wife. He must be a husband unworthy of you, who could bear the degradation of suffering this in silence. The idea of power, on either side, should be totally banished from the system: it is not sufficient that the husband should never have occasion to regret the want of it; the wife must so behave, that he may never be conscious of possessing it.

"But my Julia, if a mother's fondness deceives me not, stands not in much need of cautions like these. I cannot allow myself the idea of her wedding a man, on whom she would not wish to be dependent, or whose inclinations a temper like hers would desire to control. She will be more in danger from that softness, that sensibility of soul, which will yield perhaps too much for the happiness of both. The office of a wife includes the exertion of a friend: a good one must frequently strengthen and support that weakness, which a bad one would endeavour to overcome. There are situations, where it will not be enough to love, to cherish, to obey: she must teach her husband to be at peace with himself, to be reconciled to the world, to resist misfortune, to conquer adversity.

"Alas! my child, I am here an instructress but too well skilled! These tears, with which this paper is soiled, fell not in the presence of your father, though, now, they but trace the remembrance of what then it was my lot to feel. Think it not impossible to restrain your feelings, because they are strong. The enthusiasm of feeling will sometimes overcome distresses, which the cold heart of prudence had been unable to endure.

"But *misfortune* is not always *misery*. I have known this truth; I am proud to believe, that I have sometimes taught it to Roubigné. Thanks be to that Power, whose decrees I reverence! He often tempered the anguish of our sufferings, till there was a sort of luxury in feeling them. Then is the triumph of wedded love! — the tie that binds the happy may be dear; but that which links the unfortunate is tenderness unutterable.

"There are afflictions less easy to be endured, which your mother has not experienced: those which a husband inflicts, and the best wives feel the most severely. These, like all our sharpest calamities, the fortitude that can resist can only cure. Complainings debase her who suffers, and harden him who aggrieves. Let not a woman always look for their cause in the injustice of her lord; they may proceed from many trifling errors in her own conduct, which virtue cannot blame, though wisdom must regret. If she makes this discovery, let them be amended without a thought, if possible, at any rate without an expression, of merit in amending them. In this, and in every other instance, it must never be forgotten, that the only government allowed on our side, is that of gentleness and attraction; and that its power, like the fabled influence of imaginary beings, must be invisible to be complete.

"Above all, let a wife beware of communicating to others any want of duty or tenderness she may think she has perceived in her husband. This untwists, at once, those delicate cords, which preserve the unity of the marriage-engagement. Its sacredness is broken for ever, if third parties are made witnesses of its failings, or umpires of its disputes. It may seem almost profane in me to confess, that once, when, through the malice of an enemy, I was made, for a short time, to believe, that my Roubigné had wronged me, I durst not, even in my prayers to Heaven, petition for a restoration of his love; I prayed to be made a better wife: when I would have said a more beloved one, my utterance failed me for the word."

* * * * * *

Julia to Maria

WE HAVE got to the end of our journey; and I am now mistress of this mansion. Our journey was too short and too slow; I wished for some mechanical relief from my feelings in the rapidity of a post chaise; our progress was too stately to be expeditious, and we reached not this place, though but six leagues distant, till evening.

Methinks I have suffered a good deal; but my heart is not callous yet: else wherefore was it wrung so at leaving my father's peaceful retreat? I did not trust myself with looking back; but I was too well acquainted with the objects, not to recollect every tree from the side window as we passed. A little ragged boy, who keeps some sheep of my father's, opened the gate for us at the end of the furthermost inclosure; he pulled off his hat, which he had adorned with some gay coloured ribbands in honour of the occasion; Montauban threw money into it, and the boy followed us for some time with a number of blessings. When he turned back, methought I envied him his return. The full picture of the place we had left, rose before me; it needed all my resolution, and all my fears of offending, to prevent my weeping outright. At our dinner on the road, I was very busy, and affected to be very much pleased; La Pelliere was a lucky companion for me; you know how full she is of observation on trifles. When we approached the house, she spoke of every thing, and praised every thing; I had nothing to do but to assent.

We entered between two rows of lime-trees, at the end of which is the gate of the house, wide and rudely magnificent; its large leaves were opened to receive us by an old but fresh-looking servant, who seemed too honest to be polite, and did not show me quite so much curtesy as some mistresses would have expected. All these circumstances, however, were in a style which my friend has heard me commend; yet was I weak enough not perfectly to relish them when they happened to myself. There was a presaging gloom about this mansion, which filled my approach with terror; and when Montauban's old domestic opened the coach door, I looked upon him as a criminal might do on the messenger of death. My dreams ever since have been full of horror; and while I write these lines, the creaking of the pendulum of the great clock in the hall sounds like the knell of your devoted Julia.

I expect you to rally me on my ideal terrors. — You may remember, when we used to steal a midnight hour's conversation together, you would laugh at my foreboding of a short period to my life, and often jeeringly tell me, I was born to be a great-grand-mother in my time. I know the foolishness of this impression, though I have not yet been able to conquer it. But to me it is not the source of disquiet; I never feel more possessed of myself than at those moments when I indulge it the most. Why should I wish for long life? why should so many wish for it? Did we sit down to number the calamities of the world; did we think how many wretches there are of disease, of poverty, of oppression, of vice, (alas! I am afraid there are some even of virtue,) we should change one idea of evil, and learn to look on death as a friend.

This might a philosopher accomplish; but a Christian, Maria, can do more. Religion has taught me to look beyond dissolution. Religion has removed the darkness that covered the sepulchres of our fathers, and filled that gloomy void, which was only the retreat of hopeless affliction, with prospects, in contemplation of which, even the felicity of the world dwindles into nothing!

ADVERTISEMENT

[*MY Readers will easily perceive something particular in the place where the following letters of Savillon are found, as they are manifestly of a date considerably prior to many of the preceding. They came to my hands assorted in the manner I have now published them, probably from a view in my young friend, who had the charge of their arrangement, of keeping the correspondence of Julia, which communicated the great train of her feelings on the subjects contained in it as much undivided as possible. While I conjectured this reason for their present order, I was aware of some advantage which these papers, as relating a story, might derive from an alteration in that particular; but, after balancing those different considerations, without coming to any decision, my indolence (perhaps a stronger motive with most men than they are disposed to allow) at length prevailed, and I resolved to give them to the Public in the order they were transmitted to me from France. Many of the particulars they recount are anticipated by a perusal of the foregoing letters; but it is not so much on story, as sentiment, that their interest with the Reader must depend.*]

Savillon to Beauvaris

AFTER A very unfavourable passage, we are at last arrived at our destined port. A ship is lying along side of us, ready to sail for France, and every one on board, who can write, is now writing to some relation or friend, the hardships of his voyage, and the period of his arrival. How few has Savillon to greet with tidings! to Roubigné I have already written; to Beauvaris I am now writing; and, when I have excepted these, there is not in France a single man, to whom I am entitled to write. Yet I mean not to class them together: — to Roubigné I owe the tribute of esteem, the debt of gratitude; for you I feel something tenderer than either. Roubigné has been the guide, the father of my youth, and him I reverence as a parent: you have been the friend, the brother of my soul, and with yours it mingles as with a part of itself.

You remember the circumstances of our parting. You would not bid me adieu till the ship was getting under way. I believe you judged rightly, if you meant to spare us both; the bustle of the scene, the rattling of the sails, the noise of the sailors, had a mechanical effect on the mind, and stifled those tender feelings, which we indulge in solitude and silence. When I went to bed, I had time to indulge them. I found it vain to attempt sleeping, and scarcely wished to succeed in attempting it. About midnight, I arose and went upon deck. The wind had been fair all day, and we were then, I suppose, more than thirty leagues from the shore. I looked on the arch of heaven, where the moon pursued her course unclouded; and my ear caught no sound, except the stilly noise of the sea around me. I thought of my distance from France as of some illusive dream, and could not believe, without an effort, that it was not four-and-twenty hours since we parted. I recollected a thousand things which I should have said to you, and spoke them involuntarily in the ear of night.

There was, my friend, there was one thing which I meant to have told you at parting. Had you staid a few moments longer in the room after the seaman called us, I should have spoken it then; but you shunned being alone with me, and I could not command even words enough to tell you, that I wished to speak with you in private. Hear it now, and pity your Savillon.

Julia de Roubigné! — Did you feel that name as I do! — Even traced with my own pen, what throbbing remembrances has it raised! You are acquainted with my obligations to her father; — you have heard me sometimes talk of her; but you know not, for I tremble to tell you, the power she has acquired over the heart of your friend.

The fate of my father, as well as mutual inclination, made Roubigné his friend; for this last is of a temper, formed rather to delight in the pride of assisting unfortunate worth, than in the joy of knowing it in a better situation. After the death of my father, I became the ward of his friend's generosity; a state I should have brooked but ill, had not Julia been his daughter. From those early days, when first I knew her, I remember her friendship as making part of my existence: without her, pleasure was vapid, and sorrow, in her society, was changed into enjoyment. At that time of life, the mind has little reserve. We meant but friendship, and called it so without alarm. The love, to which at length I discovered my heart to be subject, had conquered without tumult, and become despotic under the semblance of freedom.

The misfortunes of her family first shewed me how I loved. — When her father told them the ruined state of his fortune, when he prepared them for leaving the now alienated seat of his ancestors, I was a spectator of the scene. When I saw the old man, with indignant pride, stifling the anguish of his heart, and pointing to the chaise that was to carry them from Belville, his wife, with one hand clasping her husband's, the other laid on her bosom, turning up to

87

heaven a look of resignation; his daughter, striving to check her tears, kneeling before him, and vowing her duty to his misfortunes; then did I first curse my poverty, which prevented me from throwing myself at her feet, and bidding her parents be happy with their Julia! — The luxury of the idea still rushes on my mind; — to heal the fortunes of my father's friend; to justify the ways of heaven to his saint-like wife; to wipe the tears from the eyes of his angel daughter! — Beauvaris, our philosophy is false: power and wealth are the choicest gifts of heaven; to possess them, indeed, is nothing, but thus to use them is rapture!

I had them not thus to use; but what I could, I did. I attended his family to that ancient mansion, which was now the sole property of the once opulent Roubigné. With unwearied attention, I soothed his sorrows, and humbled myself before his misfortunes, as much as I had formerly resisted dependence on his prosperity.

He felt an assiduity of my friendship, and I saw him grateful for its exertion; yet would the idea of being obliged, often rankle in his mind; and I have seen him frequently look at me with an appearance of anger, when he thought I was conscious of obliging him.

Far different was the gentle nature of his daughter. She thanked me with unfeigned gratitude for my services to her father, and seemed solicitous to compensate with her smiles, for that want of acknowledgment she observed in him.

Had my heart been free before, it was impossible to preserve its freedom now. A spectator of all those excellencies in which, though she ever possessed, her present situation alone could give full room to exert; all that sublimity of mind, which bore adversity unmoved; all that gentleness, which contrived to lighten it to her father, and smooth the rankling of his haughty soul! I applauded the election I had made, and looked on my love as a virtue.

Yet there were moments of anxiety, in which I feared the consequences of indulging this attachment. My own situation, the situation of Julia, the pride of her father, the pride which it was proper for herself to feel: — All these were present to my view, and shewed me how little I could build on hope; yet it cheated me, I know not how, and I dreamed, from day to day, of blessings which every day's reflection told me were not to be looked for.

There was, indeed, something in the scene around us, formed to create those romantic illusions. The retreat of Roubigné is a venerable pile, the remains of ancient Gothic magnificence, and the grounds adjoining to it are in that style of melancholy grandeur, which marks the dwellings of our forefathers. One part of that small estate, which is still the appendage of this once respectable mansion, is a wild and rocky dell, where tasteless wealth has never warred on nature, nor even elegance refined or embellished her beauties. The walks are only worn by the tread of the shepherds, and the banks only smoothed by the feeding of their flocks. There, too dangerous society! have I passed whole days with Julia: there, more dangerous still! have I passed whole days in thinking of her.

A circumstance, trifling in itself, added not a little to the fascination of the rest. The same good woman who nursed me, was also the nurse of Julia. She was too fond of her foster-daughter, and too well treated by her, ever to leave the fortunes of her family. To this residence she attended them when they left Belville, and here too, as at that place, had a small house and garden allotted her. It was situated at the extreme verge of that dell I have described, and was often the end of those walks we took through it together. The good Lasune, (for that is our nurse's name,) considered us her children, and treated us, in those visits to her little dwelling, with that simplicity of affection, which has the most powerful effect on hearts of sensibility. Oh! Beauvaris, methinks I see the figure of Lasune, at this moment, pointing out to your friend, with rapture in her countenance, the beauties of her lovely daughter! She places our seats together; she produces her shining platters, with fruit and milk, for our repast; she presses the smiling Julia, and will not be denied by Savillon! Am I then a thousand leagues distant?

Does Julia remember Savillon! — Should I hope that she does? — My friend, I will confess my weakness; perhaps, it is worse than weakness; I have wished — I have hoped, that I am not indifferent to her. Often have I been on the point of unloading my throbbing heart, of telling her how passionately I loved, of asking her forgiveness for my presumption. I have thought, perhaps it was vanity, that at some seasons she might have answered and blessed me; but I saw the consequences which would follow to both, and had fortitude enough to resist the impulse. A time may come, when better fortune shall entitle me to speak; when the pride of Roubigné may not blush to look on Savillon as his son.

But this is the language of visionary hope! In the mean time, I am torn from her, from France, from every connection my heart had formed; cast like a shipwrecked thing on the other side of the Atlantic, amidst a desert, of all others the most dreadful, the desert of society, with which no social tie unite me! — Where now are Roubigné's little copses, where his winding walks, his nameless rivulets? Where the ivy'd gate of his venerable dwelling, the Gothic windows of his echoing hall? — That morning, on which I set out for Paris, is still fresh on my memory. I could not bear the formality of parting, and stole from his house by day-break. As I passed that hall, the door was open; I entered to take one last look, and bid it adieu! I had sat in it with Julia the night before; the chairs we had occupied were still in their places; you know not, my friend, what I felt at the sight; there was something in the silent attitude of those very chairs, that wrung my heart beyond the power of language; and, I believe, the servant had told me that my horses waited, five or six times over, before I could listen to what he said.

═══

A gentleman has sent to ask, if my name is Savillon: if it is, he desires his compliments, and will do himself the pleasure of waiting on me. I started to hear my name thus asked for in Martinique.

═══

This gentleman is a sea-captain, a particular acquaintance of my uncle: he is more, Beauvaris, he is an acquaintance of Roubigné, has been often at Belville, has sometimes seen my Julia. — We are intimate already, and he has offered to conduct me to my uncle's house: — his horses, he says, are in waiting.

Adieu, my dearest friend! think of me often; write to me often: though you should seldom have an opportunity of conveying letters, yet write as if you had; make a journal of intelligence, and let it come when it may. Tell me every thing, though I should ask nothing. Your letters must give me back my country, and nothing is a trifle that belongs to her.

LETTER XXVII.

Savillon to Beauvaris

IT IS now a week since I reached my uncle's, during all which time I have been so much occupied in answering questions to the curiosity of others, or asking questions for the satisfaction of my own, that I have scarce had a moment left for any other employment.

I have now seized the opportunity of the rest of the family being still a-bed, to write to you an account of this uncle; of him under whose protection I am to rise into life, under whose guidance I am to thrid[12] the mazes of the world. I fear I am unfit for the task: I must unlearn feelings in which I have been long accustomed to delight: I must accommodate sentiments to conveniency, pride to interest, and sometimes even virtue itself to fashion.

But is all this absolutely necessary? — I hate to believe it. I have been frequently told so indeed; but my authorities are drawn either from men who have never entered the scene at all, or entered it, resolved to be overcome without the trouble of resistance. To think too meanly of mankind, is dangerous to our reverence of virtue.

It is supposed, that, in these wealthy islands, profit is the only medium of opinion, and that morality has nothing to do in the system; but I cannot easily imagine, that, in any latitude, the bosom is shut to those pleasures which result from the exercise of goodness, or that honesty should be always so unsuccessful as to have the sneer of the million against it. Men will not be depraved beyond the persuasion of some motive, and self-interest will often be the parent of social obligation.

12. I.e. thread.

My uncle is better fitted for judging of this question; he is cool enough to judge of it from experience, without being misled by feeling. — He believes there are many more honest dealings than honest men, but that there are more honest men than knaves every where; that common sense will keep them so, even exclusive of principle; but that all may be vanquished by adequate temptation.

With a competent share of plain useful parts, and a certain steady application of mind, he entered into commerce at an early period of life. Not apt to be seduced by the glare of great apparent advantage, nor easily intimidated from his purposes by accidental disappointment, he has held on, with some vicissitude of fortune, but with uniform equality of temper, till, in virtue of his abilities, his diligence, and his observation, he has acquired very considerable wealth. He still, however, continues the labour of the race, though he has already reached the goal; not because he is covetous of greater riches, but because the industry, by which greater riches are acquired, is grown necessary to the enjoyment of life. "I have been long," said he yesterday, "a very happy man; having had a little less time, and a little more money, than I know what to make of."

The opinion of the world he trusts but little, in his judgment of others; of men's actions he speaks with caution, either in praise or blame, and is commonly most sceptical, when those around him are most convinced: for it is a maxim with him, in questions of character, to doubt of strong evidence from the very circumstance of its strength.

With regard to himself, however, he accepts of the common opinion, as a sort of coin which passes current, though it is not always real, and often seems to yield up the conviction of his own mind in compliance with the general voice. Ever averse to splendid project in action, or splendid conjecture in argument, he contents himself with walking in the beaten track of things, and does not even venture to leave it, though he may, now and then, observe it making small deviations from reason and justice. He has sometimes, since our acquaintance began, tapped me on the shoulder, in the midst of some sentiment I was uttering, and told me, with a smile, that these were fine words, and did very well in the mouth of a young man. Yet he seems not displeased with my feeling what himself does not feel; and looks on me with a more favourable eye, that I have something about me for experience and observation to prune.

His plan of domestic œconomy is regular, but nobody is disturbed by its regularity; for he is perfectly free from that rigid attention to method, which one frequently sees in the houses of old bachelors. He has sense, or *sang-froid* enough, not to be troubled with little disarrangements, and bears with wonderful complacency, and consequently with great ease to his guests, those accidents which disturb the peace of other entertainments. Since my arrival, we have had every day something like a feast, probably from a sort of compliment which his friends meant to pay to him and to me; but at his table, in its most elevated style, the government is nearly republican; he assumes very little, either of the trouble or the dignity of a landlord, satisfied with giving a general assurance of welcome and good-humour in his aspect.

At one of those dinners was a neighbour and intimate acquaintance of my uncle, a Mr Dorville, with his wife and daughter. The young lady was seated next me, and my uncle seemed to incline, that I should be particularly pleased with her. He addressed such discourse to her, as might draw her forth to the greatest advantage: and, as he heard me profess myself a lover of music, he made her sing after dinner, till, I believe, some of the company began to be tired of their entertainment. After they were gone, he asked my opinion of Mademoiselle Dorville, in that particular style by which a man gives you to understand that his own is a very favourable one. To say truth, the lady's appearance is in her favour; but there is a jealous sort of feeling which arises in my mind, when I hear the praises of any woman but one; and from that cause, perhaps, I answered my uncle rather coldly; I saw he thought so from the reply he made: I made some awkward apology: he smiled, and said I was a philosopher.[13] Alas! he knows not how little claim I have to philosophy in that way; if, indeed, we are so often to profane that word by affixing to it the idea of insensibility.

To-day I begin business. My uncle and I are to view his different plantations, and he is to shew me, in general, the province he means to allot me. I wish for an opportunity to be assiduous in his service: till I can do something on my part, his favours are like debts upon me. It is only to a friend, like my Beauvaris, that one feels a pleasure in being obliged.

---

13. In the more common eighteenth-century sense of one who regulates his life according to the reason alone; a man not easily moved by beauty.

Savillon to Beauvaris

A THOUSAND thanks for your last letter. When you know how much I enjoyed the unwieldy appearance of the packet, with my friend's hand on the back of it, you will not grudge the time it cost you. It is just such as I wished: your scene-painting is delightful. No man is more susceptible of local attachments than I; and, with the Atlantic between, there is not a stone in France which I can remember with indifference.

Yet I am happier here than I could venture to expect. Had I been left to my own choice, I should probably have sat down in solitude, to think of the past, and enjoy my reflections; but I have been forced to do better. There is an active duty which rewards every man in the performance; and my uncle has so contrived matters, that I have had very little time unemployed. He has been liberal of instruction, and, I hope, has found me willing to be instructed. Our business, indeed, is not very intricate; but, in the simplest occupations, there are a thousand little circumstances which experience alone can teach us. In certain departments, however, I have tried projects of my own: Some of them have failed in the end, but all gave me pleasure in the pursuit. In one I have been successful beyond expectation; and in that one I was the most deeply interested, because it touched the cause of humanity.

To a man not callous from habit, the treatment of negroes, in the plantations here, is shocking. I felt it strongly, and could not forbear expressing my sentiments to my uncle. He allowed them to be natural, but pleaded necessity, in justification of those severities, which his overseers sometimes used towards his slaves. I ventured to doubt this proposition, and begged he would suffer me to try a different mode of government in one plantation, the produce of which he had already allotted to my management. He consented, though with the belief that I should succeed very ill in the experiment.[14]

I began by endeavouring to ingratiate myself with such of the salves as could best speak the language of my country; but I found this was a manner they did not understand, and that, from a white, the appearance of indulgence carried the suspicion of treachery. Most of them, to whom rigour had become habitual, took the advantage of its remitting, to neglect their work altogether; but this only served to convince me, that my plan was a good one, and that I should undoubtedly profit, if I could establish some other motive, whose impulse was more steady than those of punishment and terror.

By continuing the mildness of my conduct, I at last obtained a degree of willingness in the service of some; and I was still induced to believe, that the most savage and sullen among them had principles of gratitude, which a good master might improve to his advantage.

One slave, in particular, had for some time attracted my notice, from that gloomy fortitude with which he bore the hardships of

---

14. Awareness of the appalling conditions and treatment of African slaves was slow to dawn in Britain, although shortly before the novel's publication Edinburgh society was engaged by the case of Joseph Knight, an African purchased in Jamaica by a Scottish gentleman and brought to Scotland, where the slave claimed a right to liberty. *Julia de Roubigné* contains one of the earliest discussions of how the conditions of slaves might be ameliorated in the American colonies. Savillon's (and Mackenzie's) abolitionist views are far ahead of general opinion; the debate gathered momentum only from the mid-1780s. In 1778, the year before *Julia*'s publication, the Scottish philosopher James Beattie had written (though not published) an outspoken essay 'On the Lawfulness and Expediency of Slavery, Particularly that of the Negroes', expounding abolitionist views which he had been expressing in lectures since the 1760s. Mackenzie would almost certainly have been familiar with the briefer version of this argument which appeared in Beattie's celebrated *Essay on Truth* in 1770.

his situation. — Upon enquiring of the overseer, he told me, that this slave, whom he called Yambu, though, from his youth and appearance of strength, he had been accounted valuable, yet, from the untractable stubbornness of his disposition, was worth less money than almost any other in my uncle's possession. — This was a language natural to the overseer. I answered him, in his own style, that I hoped to improve his price some hundreds of livres. On being further informed, that several of his fellow-slaves had come from the same part of the Guinea coast with him, I sent for one of them who could speak tolerable French, and questioned him about Yambu. He told me, that, in their own country, Yambu was master of them all; that they had been taken prisoners, when fighting in his cause, by another prince, who, in one battle, was more fortunate than theirs; that he had sold them to some white men, who came in a great ship to their coast; that they were after-wards brought hither, where other white men purchased them from the first, and set them to work where I saw them; but that when they died, and went beyond the Great Mountains, Yambu should be their master again.

I dismissed the negro, and called this Yambu before me.

When he came, he seemed to regard me with an eye of perfect indifference. One who had enquired no further, would have concluded him possessed of that stupid insensibility, which Europeans often mention as an apology for their cruelties. I took his hand; he considered this a prologue to chastisement, and turned his back to receive the lashes he supposed me ready to inflict. "I wish to be the friend of Yambu," said I. He made me no answer: I let go his hand, and he suffered it to drop to its former posture. "Can this man have been a prince in Africa?" said I to myself. — I reflected for a moment. — "Yet what should he now do, if he has? — Just what I see him do. I have seen a deposed sovereign at Paris; but in Europe, kings are artificial beings, like their subjects. — Silence is the only throne which adversity has left to princes.

"I fear," said I to him, "you have been sometimes treated

harshly by the overseer; but you shall be treated so no more; I wish all my people to be happy." He looked on me now for the first time. — "Can you speak my language, or shall I call for some of your friends, who can explain what you would say to me?" "I speak no say to you," he replied in his broken French. — "And you will not be my friend?" — "No." — "Even if I deserve it?" — "You a white man." — I felt the rebuke as I ought. "But all white men are not overseers. What shall I do to make you think me a good man?" — "Use men goodly." — "I mean to do so, and you among the first, Yambu." — "Be good for Yambu's people; do your please with Yambu."

Just then the bell rung as a summons for the negroes to go to work: he made a few steps towards the door. "Would you now go to work," said I, "if you were at liberty to avoid it?" "You make go for whip, and no man love go." — "I will go along with you, though I am not obliged; for I chuse to work sometimes rather than be idle." — "Chuse work, no work at all," said Yambu. — 'Twas the very principle on which my system was founded.

I took him with me into the house when our task was over. "I wrought chuse work," said I, "Yambu, yet I did less than you." — "Yambu do chuse work then too?" — "You shall do so always," answered I; "from this moment you are mine no more!" — "You sell me other white men then?" — "No, you are free, and may do whatever you please!" — "Yambu's please no here, no this country," he replied, waving his hand, and looking wistfully towards the sea. — "I cannot give you back your country, Yambu; but I can make this one better for you. You can make it better for me too, and for your people!" "Speak Yambu that," said he eagerly, "and be good man!" — "You would not," said I, "make your people work by the whip, as you see the overseers do?" — Oh! no, no whip!" — "Yet they must work, else we shall have no sugars to buy them meat and clothing with." — (He put his hand to his brow, as if I had started a difficulty he was unable to overcome.) — "Then you shall have the command of them, and they shall work chuse work for Yambu." — He looked askance, as if he doubted the truth of what I said; I called the negro with whom I had the first conversation about him, and, pointing to Yambu, "Your master," said I, "is now free, and may leave you when he pleases!" — "Yambu no leave you," said he to the negro warmly. — "But he may accompany Yambu if he chuses." — Yambu shook his head. — "Master," said his former subject, "where we go? leave good white men and go to bad; for much bad white men in this country." — "Then if you think it better, you shall both stay; Yambu shall be my friend, and help me to raise sugars for the good of us all: you shall have no overseer but Yambu, and shall work no more than he bids you."[15] — The negro fell at my feet and kissed them; Yambu stood silent, and I saw a tear on his cheek. — "This man has been a prince in Africa!" said I to myself.

I did not mean to deceive them. Next morning I called those negroes, who had formerly been in his service, together, and told them, that, while they continued in the plantation, Yambu was to superintend their work; that if they chose to leave him and me, they were at liberty to go; and that, if found idle or unworthy, they should not be allowed to stay. He has, accordingly, ever since had the command of his former subjects, and superintended their work in a particular quarter of the plantation; and having been declared free, according to the mode prescribed by the laws of the island, has a certain portion of ground allotted him, the produce of which is his property. I have had the satisfaction of observing those men, under the feeling of good treatment, and the idea of liberty, do more than almost double their number subject to the whip of an overseer. I am under no apprehension of desertion or mutiny; they work with the willingness of freedom, yet are mine with more than the obligation of slavery.

I have been often tempted to doubt, whether there is not an

---

15. Opening quotation marks have been added to this sentence to clarify the sense.

error in the whole plan of negro servitude; and whether whites, or creoles born in the West Indies, or perhaps cattle, after the manner of European husbandry, would not do the business better and cheaper than the slaves do? The money which the latter cost at first, the sickness (often owing to despondency of mind) to which they are liable after their arrival, and the proportion that die in consequence of it, make the machine, if it may be so called, of a plantation, extremely expensive in its operations. In the list of slaves belonging to a wealthy planter, it would astonish you to see the number unfit for service, pining under disease, a burden on their master. — I am talking only as a merchant; but as a man — Good heavens! when I think of the many thousands of my fellow-creatures groaning under servitude and misery! — Great God! hast thou peopled those regions of thy world for the purpose of casting out their inhabitants to chains and torture? — No; thou gavest them a land teeming with good things, and light-ed'st up thy sun to bring forth spontaneous plenty; but the refine-ments of man, ever at war with thy works, have changed this scene of profusion and luxuriance into a theatre of rapine, of slavery, and of murder!

Forgive the warmth of this apostrophe! Here it would not be understood; even my uncle, whose heart is far from a hard one, would smile at my romance, and tell me that things must be so. Habit, the tyrant of nature and of reason, is deaf to the voice of either; here she stifles humanity, and debases the species; — for the master of slaves has seldom the soul of a man.

This is not difficult to be accounted for: — from his infancy he is made callous to those feelings which soften at once and ennoble our nature. Children must, of necessity, first exert those towards domestics, because the society of domestics is the first they enjoy; here they are taught to command, for the sake of commanding; to beat and torture, for pure amusement; — their reason and good-nature improve as may be expected.

Among the legends of a European nursery, are stories of captives delivered, of slaves released, who had pined for years in the durance of unmerciful enemies. — Could we suppose its infant audience transported to the sea-shore, where a ship laden with slaves is just landing; the question would be universal, "Who shall set these poor people free?" — The young West Indian asks his father to buy a boy for him, that he may have something to vent his spite on when he is peevish.

Methinks, too, these people lose a sort of connection, which is of more importance in life than most of the relationships we enjoy. The ancient, the tried domestic of a family, is one of its most useful members; one of its most assured supports. My friend, the ill-fated Roubigné has not one relation who has stood by him in the ship-wreck of his fortunes; but the storm could not sever from their master his faithful Le Blanc, or the venerable Lasune.

Oh, Beauvaris! I sometimes sit down alone, and, transporting myself into the little circle at Roubigné's, grow sick of the world, and hate the part which I am obliged to perform in it.

Savillon to Beauvaris

SINCE THE date of my last, is a longer period than you allow between my letters; but my time has been more than commonly occupied of late. Among other employments was that of acquiring a friend. Be not, however, jealous; my heart cannot own a second in the same degree with Beauvaris; yet is this one above the level of ordinary men. He enjoys also that privilege which misfortune bestows on the virtuous.

Among those with whom my uncle's extensive dealings have connected him, he had mentioned, with particular commendation, one Herbert, an Englishman, a merchant in one of the British West India islands. Chance brought him lately to Martinique, and I was solicitous to show every possible civility to one, who, to the claim of a stranger, added the character of a worthy and amiable man. — Prepossessed as I was in his favour, my expectations fell short of the reality. I discovered in him a delicacy and fineness of sentiment, which something beyond the education of a trader must have inspired; and I looked on him, perhaps, with the greater reverence, from the circumstance of having found him in a station where I did not expect he would be found. On a closer investigation, I perceived a tincture of melancholy enthusiasm in his mind, which, I was persuaded, was not altogether owing to

---

* *It is proper to apologise for introducing a letter so purely episodical. I might perhaps say, that it is not altogether unnecessary, as it introduces a person whose correspondent Savillon becomes at a future period: but I must once more resort to an egotism for the true reason; the picture it exhibited pleased myself, and I could not resist the desire of laying it before my readers.*

the national character, but must have arisen from some particular cause.[16] This increased my regard for him; and I could not help expressing it in the very style which was suited to its object, a quiet and still attention, sympathetic but not intrusive. He seemed to take notice of my behaviour, and looked as if he had found a person, who guessed him to be unhappy, and to whom he could talk of his unhappiness. I encouraged the idea with that diffidence, which, I believe, is of all manners the most intimate with a mind of the sort I have described; and, soon after, he took an opportunity of telling me the story of his misfortunes.

It was simple, but not the less pathetic. Inheriting a considerable fortune from his father, he set out in trade with every advantage. Soon after he was settled in business, he married a beautiful and excellent woman, for whom, from his infancy, he had conceived the tenderest attachment; and, about a year after their marriage, she blessed him with a son. But love and fortune did not long continue to smile upon him. Losses in trade, to which, though benevolence like his be more exposed, the most prudent and unfeeling are liable, reduced him, from his former affluence, to very embarrassed circumstances; and his distress was aggravated from the consideration, that he did not suffer alone, but communicated misfortune to a woman he passionately loved. Some very considerable debts remained due to him in the West Indies, and he found it absolutely necessary, for their recovery, to repair thither himself, however terrible might be a separation from his wife, now in a situation of all others the most susceptible. They parted; and she was, soon after, delivered of a girl, whose promising appearance, as well as that of her brother, was some consolation for the absence of their father.

His absence, though cruel, was necessary; and he found his affairs in such a situation, that it promised not to be long. Day after day, however, elapsed without their final settlement. The impa-

16. In the eighteenth century melancholy was known as 'The English Malady,' and was believed to be peculiarly characteristic of the nation.

tience both of his wife and him was increased by the appearance of a conclusion, which so repeatedly disappointed them, till at last he ventured to suggest, and she warmly approved, the expedient of coming out to a husband, whose circumstances prevented him from meeting her at home. She set sail with her children; but wife or children never reached the unfortunate Herbert! they perished in a storm soon after their departure from England.

You can judge of the feelings of a man who upbraided himself as their murderer. An interval of madness, he informed me, succeeded the account he received of their death. When his reason returned, it settled into a melancholy, which time has soothed, not extinguished; which indeed seems to have become the habitual tone of his mind. Yet is it gentle, though deep, in its effects; it disturbs not the circle of society around him, and few, except such as are formed to discover and to pity it, observe any thing peculiar in his behaviour. But he holds it not the less sacred to himself; and often retires from the company of those, whom he has entertained with the good humour of a well-bred man, to arrange the memorials of his much-loved Emily, and call up the sad remembrance of his former joys.

Having acquired a sort of privilege with his distress, from my acquaintance with its cause, I entered his room yesterday, when he had thus shut out the world, and found him with some letters on the table before him, on which he looked with a tear, not of anguish but of tenderness. I stopped short on perceiving him thus employed; he seemed unable to speak, but making a movement, as if he desired that I should come forward, he put two of those letters successively into my hand. They were written by his wife: the first, soon after their marriage, when some business had called him away from her into the country; and the second, addressed to him in the West Indies, where, by that time, their ill-fortune had driven him. They pleased me so much, that I asked his leave to keep them for a day or two. He would not absolutely refuse me; but said, they had never been out of his possession. I pressed him no farther: I could only read them over repeatedly, and some parts that struck most forcibly on my memory, which, you know, is pretty tenacious, I can recollect almost *verbatim*. To another it might seem odd to write such things as these; but my Beauvaris is never inattentive to the language of nature, or the voice of misfortune.

In the first letter were the following expressions:

"You know not what feelings are here, at thus, for the first time, writing to my Henry under the name of husband. A mixture of tenderness, of love, of esteem, and confidence; — a something never experienced before, is so warm in my heart, that sure it is, at this moment, more worthy of his love than ever. — Shall not this last, my Henry, notwithstanding what I have heard from the scoffers among you men? I think it will. It is not a tumultuous transport, that must suddenly disappear; but the soft still pleasure of a happy mind, that can feel its happiness, and delight in its cause.

"I have had little company since you left me, and I wish not for much. The idea of my Henry is my best companion. I have figured out your journey, your company, and your business, and filled up my hours with the picture of what they are to you.

* * * * * * *

"John has just taken away my chicken: you know he takes liberties — 'Dear heart, a leg and wing only! — Betty says, madam, the cheesecakes are excellent.' — I smiled at John's manner of pressing, and helped myself to a cheesecake. The poor fellow looked so happy — 'My master will soon return,' said he, by way of accounting for my puny dinner. He set the wine upon the table: I filled out half a glass, and began to think of you; but, in carrying it to my lips, I reproached myself that it was not a bumper. John, I believe, guessed at the correction — 'God bless him!' I heard him say, muttering as he put up the things in his basket. I sent him down with the rest of the bottle, and they are now drinking your health in the kitchen."

* * * * * * *

"My cousin Harriet has come in to see me, and is going on with the cap I was making up, while I write this by her. She is a better milliner than I, and would have altered it somewhat; but I stuck to my own way, for I heard you say you liked it in that shape. — 'It is not half so fashionable indeed, my dear,' said Harriet; but she does not know the luxury of making up a cap to please the husband one loves. This is all very foolish: is it not? but I love to tell you those trifles; it is like having you here. If you can, write to me just such a letter about you."

———

Of the other letter, I recollect some passages, such as these:

"Captain Lewson has just now been with me, but has brought no letter; and gives for reason, your having written by a ship that left the island but a few days before him, meaning the Triton, by which I got your last; but I beg to hear from you by every opportunity, especially by so friendly a hand as Lewson: it would endear a man, to whom I have reason to be grateful, much more to me, that he brought a few lines from you. — Think, my dearest Henry, that hearing from you is all that your Emily has now to expect, at least for a long, long time.

"Perhaps (as you sometimes told me in former days, when, alas! we only talked of misfortunes) we always think our present calamity the bitterest; yet, methinks, our separation is the only evil, for which I could not have found a comfort. In truth, we were not unhappy: health and strength were left us: we could have done much for one another, and for our dear little ones. I fear, my love, you thought of me less nobly than I hope I deserved: I was not to be shocked by any retrenchment from our former way of living: I could have borne even the hardships of poverty, had it left me my Henry."

* * * * * *

"Your sweetmeats arrived very safe under the care of Captain Lewson: the children have profited by them, particularly Billy, who has still some remains of the hooping-cough. He asked me, if they did not come from papa? 'And when,' said he, 'will papa come himself?' 'Papa,' cried my little Emmy, who has just learned to lisp the word. 'She never saw papa,' replied her brother, 'did she, mamma?' — I could not stand this prattle; my boy wept with me for company's sake!"

* * * * * * *

"Emmy, they tell me, will be a beauty. She has, to say truth, lovely dark blue eyes, and a charming complexion. I think there is something of melancholy in her look; but this may be only my fancy. Billy is quite different, a bold spirited child; yet he is remarkably attentive to every thing I endeavour to teach him; and can read a little already, with no other tutor than myself. I chose this task, to amuse my lonely hours; for I make it a point of duty, to keep up my spirits as well as I can. Sometimes, indeed, I droop in spite of me, especially when you seem to waver about the time of your return. Think, my love, what risks your health runs for the sake of those riches, which are of no use without it; and after all, it is chiefly in opinion, that their power of bestowing happiness consists. I am sure the little parlour, in which I now write, is more snug and comfortable, than the large room we used to receive company in formerly; and the plain meal, to which I sit down with my children, has more relish than the formal dinners we were obliged to invite them to. Return then, my dearest Henry, from those fatigues and dangers, to which, by your own account, you are obliged to be exposed. Return to your Emily's love, and the smiles of those little cherubs that wait your arrival."

Such was the wife whom Herbert lost; you will not wonder at his grief; yet, sometimes, when the whole scene is before me, I know not how, I almost envy him his tears.

It is something to endeavour to comfort him. 'Tis perhaps a selfish movement in our nature, to conceive an attachment to such a character; one that throws itself on our pity by feeling its distresses, is ever more beloved than that which rises above them. — I know, however, without farther inquiry, that I feel myself pleased with being the friend of Herbert; would we were in France, that I might make him the friend of Beauvaris!

Your last mentions nothing of Roubigné, or his family. I know he dislikes writing, and therefore am not surprised at his silence to myself. You say, in a former letter, you find it difficult to hear of them; there is a young lady in Paris, for whom the lovely Julia has long entertained a very uncommon friendship; her name is Roncilles, daughter of the president Roncilles. — Yet, on second thoughts, I would not have you visit her on purpose to make inquiry as from me; but you may fall on some method of getting intelligence of them in this line.

Do not let slip the opportunity of this ship's return to write me fully; she is consigned to a correspondent of ours, and particular care will be taken of my letters. I think, if that had been the case, with the last that arrived here, I should have found one from you on board of her. Think of me frequently, and write to me as often as our situation will allow.

Savillon to Beauvaris

I BEGIN to suspect, that the sensibility, of which young minds are proud, from which they look down with contempt, on the unfeeling multitude of ordinary men, is less a blessing than an inconvenience. — Why cannot I be as happy as my uncle, as Dorville, as all the other good people around me? — I eat, and drink, and sing, nay I can be merry, like them; but they close the account, and set down this mirth for happiness; I retire to the family of my own thoughts, and find them in weeds of sorrow.

Herbert left this place yesterday! the only man besides thee, whom my soul can acknowledge as a friend. And him, perhaps, I shall see no more: and thee! my heart droops at this moment, and I could weep, without knowing why. — Tell me, as soon as possible, that you are well and happy; there is, methinks, a languor in your last letter — or is but the livery of my own imagination, which the objects around me are constrained to wear?

Herbert was a sort of proxy for my Beauvaris; he spoke from the feelings of a heart like his. To him I could unbosom mine, and be understood; for the speaking of a common language, is but one requisite towards the dearest intercourse of society. His sorrows gave him a sacredness in my regard, that made every endeavour to serve or oblige him, like the performance of a religious duty: there was a quiet satisfaction in it, which calmed the rufflings of a sometimes troubled spirit, and restored me to peace with myself.

He has sailed for England, whither some business, material to a friend of his much-loved Emily, obliges him to return. He yields to this, I perceive, as a duty he thinks himself bound to discharge, though the sight of his native country, spoiled as it is of those blessings which it once possessed for him, must be no easy trial of his fortitude. He talks of leaving it as soon as this affair will allow him, not to return to the West Indies, (for of his business there he is now independent,) but to travel through some parts of Europe, which the employments of his younger years prevented him from visiting at an early period of life. If he goes to Paris, he has promised me to call on you. Could I be with you! — What a thought is there! — but I shall not be forgotten at the interview.

═════

I have just received yours of the third of last month. I must still complain of its shortness, though I dare not quarrel with it, as it assures me of your welfare. But get rid, I pray you, of that very bad practice, of supposing things unimportant at Martinique, because you think them so at Paris. Give me your intelligence, and allow me to be the judge of its consequence.

You are partial to your friend, when you write in such high terms of his treatment of Yambu. — We think but seldom of these things which habit has made common, otherwise we should correct many of them; there needed only to give one's feelings room on this theme, and they could prompt no other conduct than mine. Your approbation, however, is not lost upon me; the best of our resolutions are bettered by a consciousness of the suffrage of good men in their favour; and the reward is still higher, when that suffrage is from those we love.

═════

My uncle has sent to me, to help him to entertain some company who are just arrived here. He knows not what a train of thinking he calls me from — I have a little remembrancer, Beauvaris, a picture, which has hung at my bosom for some years past, that speaks such things! —

The servant again! — Mademoiselle Dorville is below, and I must come immediately. — Well then — it will be difficult for me to be civil to her — yet the girl deserves politeness. — But that picture! —

* * * * * * *

Savillon to Beauvaris

You say the letter, to which your last was an answer, was written in low spirits. I confess I am not always in high ones; not even now, though I am just returned from a little feast, where there was much mirth, and excellent wine. It was a dinner given by Dorville, on occasion of his daughter's birth-day, to which my uncle and I, among other of his friends, had been long invited. The old gentleman displayed all his wealth, and all his wit, in entertaining us: some of us thanked him for neither, though every one's complaisance obliged them to eat of his dainties, and laugh at his jests.

It is after such a scene, that one is often in a state the most stupid of any. The assumption of a character, in itself humiliating, distresses and wastes us, while the loss of so much time, like the bad fortune of a gamester, is doubly felt, when we reflect that fools have won from us. Yet it must be so in life, and I wish to overcome the spleen of repining at it.

I was again set next Mademoiselle Dorville, and had the honour of accompanying some of the songs she sung to us. A vain fellow, in my circumstances, might imagine, that the girl liked him. I believe there is nothing so serious in her mind, and I should be sorry there were. The theft of a woman's affections is not so atrocious as that of her honour; but I have often seen it more terrible than that of her life; at least if living wretchedness be worse than death; yet is it reckoned a very venial breach of confidence, to endeavour to become more than agreeable, where a man feels it impossible to repay what he may receive. Her father, I am apt to believe, has something of what is commonly called a plot upon me;

but as to him, my conscious is easy, because, the coffers of my uncle being his quarry, it matters not much if he is disappointed.

Were it not from a point of delicacy, not to run the smallest risk of being thought particular, I could sometimes be very well entertained with the society of Mademoiselle Dorville. There is a sprightliness about her, which amuses, though it is not winning; and I never found it so easy to talk nonsense to any other woman. I fancy this is always the case, where there is no chance of the heart being interested: it is perfectly so in the present case with me. Oh, Beauvaris! I have laid out more soul in sitting five minutes with Julia de Roubigné in silence, than I should in a year's conversation with this little Dorville.

The conversation of women has perhaps a charm from its weakness; but this must be, like all their other weaknesses that please us, what claims an interest in our affections, without offending our reason. I know not if there is really a sex in the soul; custom and education have established one in our idea; but we wish to feel the inferiority of the other sex, as one that does not debase, but endear it.[17]

To their knowledge, in many things, we have set limits, because it seems to encroach on the softness of their feelings, which we suppose of that retiring kind that shuns the keenness of argument or inquiry. Knowledge or learning has often this effect among men: it is even sometimes fatal to taste, if by taste is meant the effect which beauties have on ourselves, rather than the power of criticising on that which they ought to have on others.

There is a little world of sentiment made for women to move in, where they certainly excel our sex, and where our sex ought, perhaps, to be excelled by them. This is irresistibly engaging, where it is natural; but, of all affectations, that of sentiment is the most disgusting. It is, I believe, more common in France than any

---

17. Mackenzie's essay for *The Mirror*, No. 30 (8 May 1779), raises the same question, and treats it as indisputable that 'whether or not there be a sex in the soul ... there is one in manners' (*Works*, IV, p. 120).

where else; and I am not sure if it does not proceed from our women possessing the reality less. The daughter of Mons. Dorville, when she would be great, is always sentimental. I was forced to tell her to-day, that I hated sentiments, and that they spoiled the complexion. She looked in the glass, and began to ask some questions about the Italian comedy.

===

My uncle, who had staid some time behind me with Dorville, came in. He was very copious on the subject of Mademoiselle. I was perfectly of his opinion in every thing, and praised her in echo to what he said; but he had discernment enough to see an indifference in this, which, I was sorry to find, he did not like. I know not how far he meant to go, if we had been long together; but he found himself somewhat indisposed, and was obliged to go to bed.

I sat down alone, and thought of Julia de Roubigné.

My uncle is, this morning, really ill. I owe him too much, not to be distressed at this. He is uneasy about his own situation, though, I believe, without reason; but men, who, like him, have enjoyed uninterrupted health, are apt to be apprehensive. I have sent for a physician, without letting him know; for it was another effect of his good constitution, to hold the faculty in contempt. At present, I am sure, he will thank me in his heart for my precaution.

===

The doctor has been with him, and talks doubtfully; that, perhaps, is unavoidable in a science, from its nature so uncertain; for this man has really too much knowledge to wish to seem wiser.

===

I find I must conclude this letter, as the ship, by which I am to send it, is within a quarter of an hour of sailing. Would it had been a few days later! a few days might do much in a fate like mine. — I cannot express that sort of doubt and fear, which the look of futurity, at this moment, gives me.

Do not, for heaven's sake, do not fail to write to me about the situation of Roubigné and his family. I know his unwillingness to write, and decorum prevents (is it vanity to think so?) his daughter; therefore I addressed my last letter to Madame de Roubigné; but even when I shall receive her answer, it will not say enough. You know what my heart requires; do not disappoint it.*

---

* *There are no letters, in this collection, of a later date, from Savillon to Beauvaris. The person who at first arranged them, seems to intend to account for this, by the following note on the outside of the preceding one, written in a hand of which I see little jottings on several of the letters, "Beauvaris died 5th April, a few days after the receipt of this."*

Julia de Roubigné to Maria de Roncilles

You MUST not expect to hear from me as often as formerly; we have, here, an even tenor of days, that admits not of much description. Comedies and romances, you know, always end with a marriage, because, after that, there is nothing to be said.

But I have reason to be angry with you for finding so little to say at Paris; though, I believe, the fault is in myself, or rather in your idea of me. You think I am not formed to relish those articles of intelligence, which are called news in your great town: the truth is, I have often heard them with very little relish; but I know you have wit enough to make them pleasant if you would; and even if you had not, do but write any thing, and I shall read it with interest.

You flatter me by your praises of the *naïveté*, in the picture I drew of our party of pleasure.[18] God knows, I have no talent that way; yet the groupe was fantastic enough, and, though I felt quite otherwise than merry next morning when I wrote to you, yet I found a sort of pleasure in describing it. There is a certain kind of trifling, in which a mind not much at ease can sometimes indulge itself. One feels an escape, as it were, from the heart, and is fain to take up with lighter company. It is like the theft of a truant-boy, who goes to play for a few minutes while his master is asleep, and throws the chiding for his task upon futurity.

We have very different company at present. Madame de

18. Artlessness: the correspondence consistently stresses Julia's unworldiness and absence of calculation; the impression is complicated, however, by the knowledge that this message is mediated for the reader through the consciousness of Julia herself.

Sancerre has been here these three days. Her husband was an acquaintance of Mons. de Montauban in Spain, and you will remember, we used to be of her parties in town; so she is a guest of both sides of the house, though, I believe, no great favourite of either. She is a wit, you know, and says abundance of good things; and will say any thing, provided it be witty. Here, indeed, we give her so little opportunity, that her genius is almost famished for want of subject. At Paris, I remember her surrounded by men of letters; they praised her learning, and to us she seemed wonderful both as a scholar and a critic; but here, when I turn the discourse on books, she chuses to talk of nothing but the *beau monde*. Her descriptions, however, are diverting enough, and, I believe, she is not the worse pleased with me, that I can only hear them without being able to answer; for I think, if there is a member of our society she dislikes, it is that relation of the count, whom I mentioned to you in my last, Mons. de Rouillé, who is come to spend some weeks here. From the account of his vivacity, which I received from his kinsman, I thought Madame de Sancerre would have thought it a piece of high good fortune to have met him here; but, I see, I mistook the thing; and that she would relish his company better, if he were as stupid as the rest of us. I am of a different opinion, and begin to like him much; the better that I was prepared to be somewhat afraid of him: but I find in him nothing to be feared; on the contrary, he is my very safest barrier against the sometimes too powerful brilliancy of the lady.

Rouillé is constitutionally happy; but his vivacity, though it seems to be constant, does not appear to be unfeeling. It is not the cheerfulness of an unthinking man, who is ready to laugh on all occasions, without leave of his reason, or, what is worse, of his humanity: some such people I have seen, whose mirth was like the pranks of a madman, and, if not of consequence enough to excite anger or fear, was entitled to our compassion. — Rouillé has the happy talent of hitting that point, where sentiment mingles with good humour. His wit, except when forced into opposition by the petulance of others, is ever of that gentle kind from which we have nothing to dread; that sports itself on the level of ordinary understandings, and pleases, because it makes no one displeased with himself. Even the natural gravity of Montauban yields to the winning liveliness of Rouillé; and, though the first seems to feel a little awkwardness in the attempt, yet he often comes down from the loftiness of his own character, to meet the pleasantry of the other's.

Do not rally me on the savour of matrimony in the observation, if I venture to say, that Montauban seems to have resumed somewhat of his former dignity. Think not that I suspect the smallest diminution of his affection; but now when the ease of the husband has restored him to his native character — I know not what I would say — Believe me, I mean nothing at all. I have the greatest reason to be satisfied and happy.

At present, I believe, he is now and then out of humour with this visitant of ours, Madame de Sancerre; and, it may be, thrown into somewhat of a severity in his manner, from the observation of an opposite one in her. When she utters, as she does pretty often, any joke at which she laughs heartily herself, I laugh, sometimes with good will, but oftener (out of complaisance) without; Rouillé laughs, and is ready with his jest in returns; but Montauban looks graver than ever. Indeed, there is no resourse for one who cannot laugh at a jest, but to look grave at it.

I wish my Maria could have accepted of the invitation he communicated by me some time ago. I think I should have shown him, in my friend, a liveliness that would not have displeased him. Could you still contrive to come, while Rouillé is here, you must be charmed with one another. It would give me an opportunity of making up to you, for the many dull letters I have obliged you to read: but you taxed yourself early with my correspondence; it was then, perhaps, tolerable; it has of late been a mere collection of egotisms, — the egotism, too, of a mind ill at ease. But I have given up making apologies or acknowledgments to you; they are only for common obligations: mine is a debt beyond their quittance.

Montauban to Segarva

I AM now three letters in your debt; yet the account of correspondence used formerly to be in my favour. The truth is, that of facts I have nothing to write, and of sentiments almost as little. Of the first, my situation here in the country deprives me; and of the last, that quiet sort of state I have got into is little productive. When I was unhappy as the lover of Julia, or first happy as her husband, I had theme enough, and to spare. I can tell you, that I am happy still; but it is a sort of happiness that would not figure in narration. I believe my Julia is every thing that a good wife should be; I hope I am a good husband. I am neither young nor old enough for a doating one.

You will smile, and look back to certain letters and notes of mine, written some four or five months ago. I do not know why I should be ashamed of them. Were Segarva to marry, he would write such letters for a while, and there never was a man who could write such letters long. If there were, I am not sure if I should wish to be that man. — When we cannot be quite so happy as others, our pride naturally balances the account; it shows us, that we are wiser.

Rouillé, who has been here for a week or two, is of a different opinion; he holds the happiest man to be ever the wisest. You know Rouillé's disposition, which was always too much in the sun for us; but the goodness of his heart, and the purity of his honour, are above the rest of his character. With this prepossession in his favour, I hear him laugh at me without resentment; and, by and bye, he steals upon me, till I forget myself, and laugh with him. I am sometimes gay; but I feel a sort of trouble in gaiety.

It is exactly the reverse with Rouillé: he can be serious, when he means to be so; but, if we mean nothing, he is gay and I am serious.

My wife is neither the one nor t'other; there is something about her too gentle for either: but, I think, her pensive softness deserts more readily to Rouillé's side than to mine, though one should imagine his manner the most distant from her's of the two. Rouillé jokes me on this; he calls her the middle stage between us; but says, it is up-hill towards my side. "A solitary castle, and a still evening," said he, "would make a Julia of me; but to be Montauban, I must have a fog and a prison."

Perhaps, if we consider matters impartially, these men have the advantage of us; the little cordialities of life are more frequently in use than its greater and more important duties. Somebody, I think, has compared them to small pieces of coin, which, though of less value than the large, are more current amongst them: but the parallel fails in one respect; a thousand of those *livres* do not constitute a *louis*;[19] and I have known many characters possessed of all that the first could give, whose minds were incapable of the last. In this number, however, I mean not to include Rouillé.

We have another guest, who illustrates my meaning better, the widow of Sancerre, whom you introduced to my acquaintance, a long time ago, in Spain. She was then nothing, for Sancerre considered all women nothing; and took care, that during his life, she should be no exception to the rule. He died; she regained her freedom; and she uses it as one to whom it had been long denied. She is just fool enough to be a wit, and carries on a perpetual crusade against sense and seriousness. I bear with her very impatiently: she plagues me, I believe, the more. My wife smiles, Rouillé laughs at me; I am unable to laugh, and ashamed to be angry; so I remain silent and stupid.

Sometimes I cease to think of her, and blame myself. Why should I allow this spleen of sense to disqualify me for society?

---

19. Montauban's Christian name is Louis; Mackenzie perhaps intends the pun as a further ominous indication of the Count's pride.

once or twice I almost uttered things against my present situation — Julia loves me; I know she does: she has that tenderness and gratitude which will secure her affection to a husband, who loves her as I do; but she must often feel the difference of disposition between us. Had such a man as Rouillé been her husband — not Rouillé neither, though she seems often delighted with his good humour, when I cannot be pleased with it — We are neither of us such a man as the writer of a romance would have made a husband for Julia — There is, indeed, a pliability in the minds of women in this article, which frequently gains over opinion to the side of duty. — Duty is a cold word — No matter, we will canvass it no farther. I know the purity of her bosom, and, I think, I am not unworthy of its affection.

Her father I see much seldomer than I could wish; but he is greatly altered of late. Since the time of his wife's death, I have observed him to droop apace; but Julia says, that the distress of their circumstances kept up in him a sort of false spirit, which, when they were disembarrassed, left him to sink under reflection. His faculties, I can easily perceive, are not in that vigour they were wont to be; yet his bodily strength does not much decline, and he seems more contented with himself than when he was in full possession of his abilities. We wish him to live with us; but he has constantly refused our request, and it is a matter of delicacy to press him on that point. We go to see him sometimes: he receives us with satisfaction, not ardour: violent emotions of every kind appear to be quenched in him. It creates, methinks, a feeling of mingled complacency and sadness, to look on the evening of a life and of a character like Roubigné's.

Shall I not see you here some time this autumn? You gave a sort of promise, and I need you more than ever. I want the society of some one, in whose company I can be pleased without the tax of thinking that I am silly for being so.

Julia to Maria

I HAVE just now received a piece of intelligence, which I must beg my Maria instantly to satisfy me about. Le Blanc, my father's servant, was here a few hours ago, and, among other news, informed Lisette, that a nephew of his, who is just come with his master from Paris, met Savillon there, whom he perfectly remembered, from having seen him in his visits to his uncle at Belville. The lad had no time for enquiry, as his master's carriage was just setting off, when he observed a chaise drive up to the door of the hotel, with a gentleman in it, whom he knew to be Savillon, accompanied by a valet de chambre, and two black servants on horseback.

Think, Maria, what I feel at this intelligence! — Yet why should it alarm me? — Alas! you know this poor, weak, throbbing heart of mine! I cannot, if I would, hide it from you. — Find him out, for heaven's sake, Maria; tell me — yet what now is Savillon to your Julia? — No matter — do any thing your prudence may suggest; only satisfy[20] me about the fate of this once dear — Again! I dare not trust myself on the subject — Monsieur de Montauban! — Farewell!

Delay not a moment to answer this. —

Yet do not write till you have learned something satisfactory.

At any rate, write me speedily. —

I have forgotten the name of the hotel where the lad met him; it was situated in the Ruë St Anne.

---

20. Mackenzie's text has 'sasisfy'.

Montauban to Segarva

MY WIFE (that word must often come across the narration of a married man) has been a good deal indisposed of late. You will not joke me on this intelligence, as such of my neighbours as I have seen have done: it is not, however, what they say, or you may think; her spirits droop more than her body; she is thoughtful and melancholy when she thinks she is not observed; and, what pleases me worse, affects to appear otherwise, when she is. I like not this sadness, which is conscious of itself. — Yet, perhaps, I have seen her thus before our marriage, and have rather admired this turn of mind than disapproved of it; but now I would not have her pensive — nor very gay neither. — I would have nothing about her, methinks, to stir a question in me whence it arose. She should be contented with the affection she knows I bear for her. I do not expect her to be romantically happy, and she has no cause for uneasiness — I am not uneasy neither — yet I wish her to conquer this melancholy.

I was last night abroad at supper: Julia was a-bed before my return. I found her lute lying on the table, and a music-book open by it. I could perceive the marks of tears shed on the paper, and the air was such as might encourage their falling: sleep, however, had overcome her sadness, and she did not awake when I opened the curtains to look on her. When I had stood some moments, I heard her sigh strongly through her sleep, and presently she muttered some words, I know not of what import. I had sometimes heard her do so before, without regarding it much; but there was something that roused my attention now. I listened; she sighed again, and again spoke a few broken words; at last, I heard her plainly pronounce the name *Savillon* two or three times over, and each time it was accompanied with sighs so deep, that her heart seemed bursting as it heaved them. I confess the thing struck me; and, after musing on it some time, I resolved to try a little experiment this day at dinner, to discover whether chance had made her pronounce this name, or if some previous cause had impressed it on her imagination. I knew a man of that name at Paris, when I first went thither, who had an office under the intendant of the marine. I introduced some conversation on the subject of the fleet, and said, in an indifferent manner, that I had heard so and so from my old acquaintance Savillon. She spilt some soup she was helping me to at the instant; and stealing a glance at her, I saw her cheeks flushed into crimson.

I have been ever since going the round of conjecture on this incident. I think I can recollect once, and but once, her father speak of a person called Savillon residing abroad, from whom he had received a letter; but I never heard Julia mention him at all. I know not why I should have forborne asking her the reason of her being so affected at the sound; yet, at the moment I perceived it, the question stuck in my throat. I felt something like guilt hang over this incident altogether — it is none of mine then — nor of Julia's neither, I trust — and yet, Segarva, it has touched me nearer, much nearer than I should own to any one but you.

———

Nine at night.

Upon looking over what I had written in the afternoon, I had almost resolved to burn this letter, and write another; but it strikes me as insincerity to a friend like Segarva, not to trust him with the very thought of the moment, weak as it may be.

I begin now to be ashamed of the effect that trifle, I mentioned above, had upon me. Julia is better, and has been singing to me the old Spanish ballad, which you sent us lately. I am delighted with those antient national songs, because there is a simplicity and an expression in them, which I can understand. Adepts in music are pleased with more intricate compositions; and they talk more of the pleasure than they feel; and others talk after them without feeling at all.

* * * * * *

Savillon to Herbert

I AM here in Paris, and fulfil the promise, which your friendship required of me, to write to you immediately on my arrival.

Alas! my reception is not such as I looked for. He, whom alone my arrival should have interested, my ever faithful Beauvaris! — he meets me not — we shall never meet — he died, while I was imagining fond things of our meeting!

Gracious God! what have I done, that I should be always thus an outcast from society? When France was dear to me as life itself, my destiny tore me from her coast; now, when I anticipated the pleasures of my return, is this the welcome she affords me?

Forlorn and friendless as my early days were, I complained not while Beauvaris was mine: he was wholly mine, for his heart was not made for the world. Naturally reserved, he shrunk early from its notice; and, when he had lived to judge of its sentiments, he wished not to be in the list of its friends.

His extreme modesty, indeed, was an evil in his fate; because it deprived him of that protection and assistance which his situation required. Those who might have been patrons of his merit, had not time to search for talents, which his bashfulness obscured. His virtues even suffered imputations from it: shy, not only of intimacy, but even of opinion and sentiment, persons, whose situation seemed to entitle them to his confidence, complained of his coldness and indifference; and he was accused of want of feeling from what, in truth, was an excess of sensibility. This jewel, undiscovered by others, was mine. From infancy, each was accustomed to consider his friend but a better part of himself; and, when the heart of either was full, talking to the other was but unloading it in soliloquy.

Forgive me, my dear Herbert, for thus dwelling on the subject. The only sad comfort I have now left me, is to think of his worth: it is a privilege I would not waste on common minds, to hear me on this theme; yours can understand it.

Why was I absent from Paris? Too much did the latter days of Beauvaris require me! They saw him struggling with poverty as well as sickness; yet the last letter he wrote to me confessed neither; and some little presents, the produce of Martinique, which I sent him, he would not convert into money, because they came from me.

I am now sitting in the room in which he died! — On that paltry bed lay the head of Beauvaris — On this desk whereon I write, he wrote — Pardon me a while — I am unable to go on.

====

It is from the indulgence of sorrow, that we first know a respite from affliction. I have given a loose to my grief, and I feel the relief, which my tears have afforded me. I am now returned to my hotel, and am able to recollect myself.

I have not yet seen any acquaintance of Mons. de Roubigné; this blow, indeed, did not allow me leisure or spirits for inquiry; I feel as if I were in a foreign land, and am almost afraid of the noise and bustle I hear in the streets. I have sent, however, offering a visit to a young lady, of whom I shall be able to get intelligence of Roubigné's family; but my messenger is not yet returned.

====

He has found her, and she has appointed me to come to her to-morrow morning. You cannot imagine what a flutter the expectation of this visit has thrown me into: I am not apt to stand in awe of presages, but I could be very weak that way at this moment. My man, who possesses a happy vivacity, brought me in, after dinner, a bottle of Burgundy, which, he said, the maitre d' hotel assured him was excellent. I have drunk three-fourths of it, by way of medicine; it has made my head somewhat dizzy, but my heart is as heavy as before.

What a letter of egotism have I written! but you have taught me to give vent to my feelings, by the acquaintance you have allowed me with yours. To speak one's distresses to the unfeeling, is terrible; even to ask the alms of pity is humiliating; but to pour our griefs into the bosom of a friend, is but committing to him a pledge above the trust of ordinary men.

Do not, I beseech you, forget your design of travelling into France this season! yet why should I ask this? I know not where fortune may lead me! it cannot, however, place me in a situation where the friendship of Herbert shall be forgotten.

P.S. I direct this for you at London, as, I think, you must be there by this time. Your answer will find me here; let it be speedy.

Savillon to Herbert

BEAR WITH me, Herbert, bear with me. The first use I make of
that correspondence which you desired, is to pour out my miseries
before you! but you can hear them — You have known what it is
to love, and to despair as I do.

When I told you my Beauvaris was no more, I thought I had
exhausted the sum of distress, which this visit to Paris was to give
me. I knew not then what fate had prepared for me — that Julia,
on whom my doating heart had rested all its hopes of happiness —
that Julia is the wife of another!

All but this I could have borne; the loss of fortune, the decay of
health, the coldness of friends, might have admitted of hope; here
only was despair to be found, and here I have found it!

Oh, Herbert! she was so interwoven with my thoughts of futurity, that life now fades into a blank, and is not worth the keeping;
— but I have a use for it; I will see her yet at least — Wherefore
should I wish to see her? — Yet, methinks, it is now the only
object that can prompt a wish in me.

When I visited that lady, that Maria de Roncilles, whom I
knew to be the dearest of her friends, she seemed to receive me with
confusion; her tongue could scarce articulate the words that told
me of Julia's marriage! She mentioned something too of having
heard of mine. — I am tortured every way with conjecture —
my brain scarce holds its recollection — Julia de Roubigné is
married to another!

I know not what I said to this friend of her's at first; I remember
only, that when I had recovered a little, I begged her to convey a
letter from me to Julia; she seemed to hesitate in her consent; but

she did at last consent. Twice have I written, and twice have I burnt what I had written — I have no friend to guide, to direct — not even to weep to!

===

At last I have finished that letter; it contains the last request which the miserable Savillon has to make. This one interview past, and my days have nothing to mark them with anxiety or hope.

===

I am now more calmly wretched; the writing of that letter has relieved, for a while, my swelling heart. I went with it myself to Mademoiselle de Roncilles; she was abroad, so I left it without seeing her. You can judge of my feelings; I wondered at the indifference of the faces I met with in my way; they had no cares to cloud them, none at least like Savillon's — Why of all those thousands am I the most wretched?

I am returned to my hotel. I hear the voices of my servants below: they are telling, I suppose, the adventures of their voyage. I can distinguish the voice of my man, and his audience are merry around him. — Why should he not jest? he knows not what his master suffers.

Something like a stupid sleepiness oppresses me: last night I could not sleep. Where are now those luxurious slumbers, those wandering dreams of future happiness? — Never shall I know them again! — Good night, my Herbert! — It is something still to sleep and to forget them.

LETTER XXXVIII.

Julia to Maria

WHAT DO you tell me! Savillon in Paris! unmarried, unregarded, raving of Julia! Hide me from myself, Maria! hide me from myself! Am I not the wife of Montauban? —

Yes, and I know that character which, as the wife of Montauban, I have to support: her husband's honour and her own, are in the breast of Julia. My heart swells, while I think on the station in which I am placed. — Relentless honour! thou triest me to the uttermost; thou enjoinest me to think no more of such a being as Savillon.

But can I think of him no more? — Cruel remembrances! — thou too, my friend, betrayest me; you dare not trust me with the whole scene; but you tell me enough. — I see him, I see him now! He came, unconscious of what fortune had made of me; he came elate with the hopes of sharing with his Julia that wealth which propitious Heaven had bestowed on him. — She is married to another! — I see him start back in amazement and despair; his eyes wild and haggard, his voice lost in the throb of astonishment! He thinks on the shadows which his fond hopes had reared — the dreams of happiness! — Say not that he wept at the thought. — Had those tears fallen upon Julia's grave, memory! thou could'st not thus have stung me. But, perhaps, gentle as his nature is, he was not weak enough to be overcome by the thought. Could he but think of me with indifference — Tell him, Maria, what a wretch I am: a wife, without a wife's affection, to whom life has lost its relish, and virtue its reward. Let him hate me, I deserve his scorn — yet, methinks, I may claim his pity.

The daughter of Roubigné, the wife of Montauban! I will not

bear to be pitied. No; I will stifle the grief that would betray me, and be miserable without a witness. This heart shall break, this proud heart, without suffering a sigh to relieve it.

Alas! my friend, it will not be. — That picture, Maria, that picture! — Why did I not banish it from my sight? too amiable Savillon! Look there, look there! in that eye there is no scorn, no reproach to the unhappy Julia: mildness and melancholy! — We were born to be miserable! — Think'st thou, Maria, that at this moment — it is possible — he is gazing thus on the resemblance of one, whose ill-fated rashness has undone herself and him! — Will he thus weep over it as I do? — Will he pardon my offences, and thus press it? — I dare not: this bosom is the property of Montauban. — Tears are all I have to bestow. Is there guilt in those tears? Heaven knows I cannot help weeping.

———

I was interrupted by the voice of my husband, giving some orders to his servant at the door of my apartment. He entered with a look of gaiety; but, I fear, by the change of his countenance, that he observed my tears. I clapped on my hat, to hide them, and told him, as well as I could, that I was going to walk. He suffered me to leave him, without any further question. I strolled I knew not whither, till I found myself by the side of a little brook, about a quarter of a mile's distance from the house. The stillness of noon, broken only by the gentle murmurings of the water, and the quiet hum of the bees, that hung on the wild flowers around it; these gave me back myself, and allowed me the langour of thought; my tears fell without control, and almost without distress. I would have looked again on the picture of Savillon, for I could then have trusted myself with the sight of it; but I had left it behind in my chamber. The thoughts of its being seen by my husband gave wings to my return. I hope he missed it; for I found it lying, as I had left it, on my dressing table, in the midst of some letters of compliment, which had been thrown carelessly there the day before; and when I went down stairs, I discovered nothing in his behaviour that should have followed such a discovery. On the contrary, I think he seemed more pleased than usual, and was particularly attentive to me. I felt his kindness a reproach, and my endeavours to return it sat awkwardly upon me. There was a treachery, methought, in my attempts to please him; and, I fear, the greater ease I meant to assume in making those attempts, I gave them only more the appearance of constraint.

What a situation is mine! to wear the appearance of serenity, while my heart is wretched; and the dissimulation of guilt, though my soul is unconscious of a crime! — There is something predictive in my mind, that tells me I shall not long be thus; but I am sick of conjecture, as I am bereft of hope, and only satisfy myself with concluding, that, in the most fateful lives, there is still a certain point, where the maze of destiny can bewilder no more!

Montauban to Segarva

SEGARVA! --- but it must be told — I blush even telling it to thee. — Have I lived to this! that thou shouldst hear the name of Montauban coupled with dishonour!

I came into my wife's room yesterday morning, somewhat unexpectedly. I observed she had been weeping, though she put on her hat to conceal it, and spoke in a tone of voice affectedly indifferent. Presently she went out, on pretence of walking; I staid behind, not without surprise at her tears, though, I think, without suspicion; when turning over (in the careless way one does in musing) some loose papers on her dressing-table, I found the picture of a young man in miniature, the glass of which was still wet with the tears she had shed on it. I have but a confused remembrance of my feelings at the time; there was a bewildered pause of thought, as if I had waked in another world. My faithful Lonquillez happened to enter the room at that moment; "Look there," said I, holding out the picture, without knowing what I did; he held it in his hand, and, turning it, read on the back *Savillon.* I started at that sound, and snatched the picture from him. I believe he spoke somewhat, expressing his surprise at my emotion; I know not what it was, nor what my answer: — He was retiring from the chamber — I called him back. — "I think," said I, "thou lovest thy master, and would serve him if thou could'st?" — "With my life!" answered Lonquillez. The warmth of his manner touched me: I think I laid my hand on my sword. — "Savillon!" I repeated the name. — "I have heard of him," said Lonquillez. — "Heard of him!" — "I heard Le Blanc talk of him a few days ago." — "And what did he say of him?" — "He said, he had heard of this gentleman's arrival from the West Indies, from his own nephew, who had just come from Paris: That he remembered him formerly, when he lived with his master at Belville, the sweetest young gentleman, and the handsomest in the province." — My situation struck me at that instant: I was unable to enquire further. After some little time, Lonquillez left the room; I knew not that he was gone, till I heard him going down stairs. I called him back a second time; he came: I could not speak. — "My dear master!" said Lonquillez — It was the accent of a friend, and it overcame me.

"Lonquillez," said I, "your master is most unhappy! — Canst thou think my wife is false to me?" — "Heaven forbid!" said he, and started back in amazement. "It may be I wrong her; but to dream of Savillon, to keep his picture, to weep over it." — "What shall I do, Sir?" said Lonquillez. — "You see I am calm," I returned, "and will do nothing rashly: Try to learn from Le Blanc every thing he knows about this Savillon; Lisette, too, is silly, and talks much. I know your faith, and will trust your capacity; get me what intelligence you can, but beware of showing the most distant suspicion." We heard my wife below; I threw down the picture where I had found it, and hastened to meet her. As I approached her, my heart throbbed so violently, that I durst not venture the meeting. My dressing-room door stood a-jar; I slunk in there, I believe, unperceived, and heard her pass on to her chamber. I would have called Lonquillez to have spoken to him again; but I durst not then, and have not found an opportunity since.

I saw my wife soon after; I counterfeited as well as I could, and, I think, she was the most embarrassed of the two; she attempted once or twice to bring in some apology for her former appearance, complained of having been ill in the morning, that her head had ached, and her eyes been hot and uneasy.

=====

She came herself to call me to dinner. We dined alone, and I marked her closely: I saw (by Heaven, I did!) a fawning solicitude to please me; an attempt at the good humour of innocence, to cover the embarrassment of guilt. I should have observed it — I am sure I should — even without a key; as it was, I could read her soul to the bottom. — Julia de Roubigné! the wife of Montauban! — Is it not so?

═══

I have had time to think. — You will recollect the circumstances of our marriage; her long unwillingness, her almost unconquerable reluctance. — Why did I marry her?

Let me remember. I durst not trust the honest decision of my friend, but stole into this engagement without his knowledge; I purchased her consent, I bribed, I bought her; bought her, the leavings of another! — I will trace this line of infamy no further: there is madness in it!

Segarva, I am afraid to hear from you; yet write to me, write to me freely. If you hold me justly punished — yet spare me when you think on the severity of my punishment.

Montauban to Segarva

LONQUILLEZ HAS not slept on his post, and chance has assisted his vigilance. Le Blanc came hither the morning after our conversation: Lonquillez managed his enquiry with equal acuteness and caution; the other told everything as the story of an old man. He smiled, and told it. He knew not that he was delivering the testimony of a witness — that the fate of his former mistress hung on it!

This Savillon lived at Belville from his earliest youth, the companion of Julia, though a dependant on her father. When they were forced to remove thence, he accompanied their retreat, the only companion of Roubigné, whom adversity had left him to comfort it — but he had his reward; the company of the daughter often supplied the place of her father's. He was her master in literature, her fellow-scholar in music and painting, and they frequently planned walks in concert, which they afterwards trod together. Le Blanc has seen them there, listening to the song of the nightingale.

I am to draw the conclusion. All this might be innocent, the effects of early intimacy and friendship; and, on this supposition, might rest the quiet of an indifferent husband. But why was this intimacy, this friendship, so industriously concealed from me? The name of Savillon never mentioned, except in guilty dreams? while his picture was kept in her chamber, for the adultery of the imagination! Do I triumph while I push this evidence? — Segarva! whither will it lead me?

The truth rises upon me, and every succeeding circumstance points to one conclusion. Lisette was to-day of a junketting party, which Lonquillez contrived for the entertainment of his friend Le Blanc. Mention was again made of old stories, and Savillon was a person of the drama. The wench is naturally talkative, and she was then in spirits, from company and good cheer. Le Blanc and she recollected interviews of their young mistress and this handsome *elevé* of her father.[21] They were, it seems, nursed by the same woman, that old Lasune, for whom Julia procured a little dwelling, and a pension of four hundred livres, from her unsuspecting husband. "She loved them," said Le Blanc, "like her own children, and they were like brother and sister to each other." — "Brother and sister, indeed!" said Lisette. — She was more sagacious, and had observed things better. — "I know what I know," said she; "but, to be sure, those things are all over now, and I am persuaded, my mistress loves no man so well as her own husband. What signifies what happened so long ago, especially while Mons. de Montauban knows nothing about the matter?"

These were her words: Lonquillez repeated them thrice to me. Were I a fool, a driveller, I might be satisfied no doubt and be uneasy; it is Montauban's to see his disgrace, and, seeing, to revenge it.

———

Lonquillez has been with me; his diligence is indefatigable: but he feels for the honour of his master, and, being a Spaniard, is entitled to share it.

He went with Le Blanc to see Lasune, whom that old man, it seems, never fails to visit when he is here. Lonquillez told her, that Le Blanc had news for her about her foster-son. "Of my dear Savillon?" cried she. — "Yes," said Le Blanc: "You will have heard, that he arrived from abroad some weeks ago; and I am told, that he is worth a power of money, which his uncle left him in the West Indies." — "Bless him! Heavens bless him!" cried Lasune:

---

21. Pupil, *protégé.*

"Then I may see him once more before I die, — You never saw him," turning to Lonquillez, "but Le Blanc remembers him well; the handsomest, sweetest, best conditioned — Your mistress and he have often sat on that bench there — Lord pity my forgetfulness! it was far from this place; but it was just such a bench — and they would prefer poor Lasune's little treat, to all the fine things at my master's; and how he would look on my sweet child! — Well, well, destiny rules every thing; but there was a time when I thought I should have called her by another name than Montauban." — Lonquillez was too much struck with her words to appear unaffected by them; she observed his surprise. "You think no harm, I hope," said she. He assured her he did not. "Nay, I need not care, for that part, who hears me; yet some folks might think it odd: But we are all friends here, as we may say, and neither of you, I know, are tale-bearers, otherwise I should not prattle as I do; especially, as the last time I saw my lady, when I asked after her foster-brother, she told me, I must not speak of him now, nor talk of the meetings they used to have at my house."

Such were her words: the memory of Lonquillez is faithful, and he was interested to remember. — I drew my breath short, and muttered vengeance. The good fellow saw my warmth, and tried to moderate it. "It is a matter, Sir," said he, "of such importance, that, if I may presume to advise, nothing should be believed rashly. If my mistress loves Savillon, if he still answers her fondness, they will surely write to each other. I commonly take charge of the letters for the post; if you can find any proof that way, it cannot lie nor deceive you."

I have agreed to his proposal. — How am I fallen, Segarva, when such artifices are easy to me! — But I will not pause on trivial objections — the fate of Montauban is set upon this cast, and the lesser moralities must speak unheeded.

Montauban to Segarva

IT IS something to be satisfied of the worst. I have now such proof, Segarva! — Enquiry is at an end, and vengeance is the only business I have left. Before you can answer this — the infamy of your friend cannot be erased, but it shall be washed in blood!

Lonquillez has just brought me a letter from my wife to a Mademoiselle de Roncilles, a bosom friend of hers at Paris. He opened it, by a very simple operation, without hurting its appearance. It consisted only of a few hurried lines, desiring her to deliver an enclosed letter to Savillon, and to take charge of his answer. — That letter now lies before me. — Read it, Segarva — thou wilt wish to stab her while thou read'st it — but Montauban has a dagger too.

"I know not, Sir, how to answer the letter my friend Mademoiselle de Roncilles has just sent me from you. *The intimacy of our former days I still recal, as one of the happiest periods of my life.* The friendship of Julia you are certainly still entitled to, and might claim, without the suspicion of impropriety, though fate has now thrown her into *the arms of another.* There would then be no occasion for this secret interview, which, I confess, I cannot help dreading; but as you urge the impossibility of your visiting Mons. de Montauban, without betraying *emotions, which, you say, would be dangerous to the peace of us all*, conjured as I am by those motives of compassion, which my heart is, perhaps, but too susceptible of for my own peace, I have at last, *not without a feeling like remorse*, resolved to meet you on Monday next, at the house of our old nurse Lasune, *whom I shall prepare for the purpose, and on whose fidelity I can perfectly rely.* I hope you will give me credit for that remembrance of Savillon, which your letter, rather unjustly, denies me, when you find me agreeing to this measure of imprudence, of danger, *it may be of guilt*, to mitigate the distress which I have been unfortunate enough to give him."

———

I feel, at this moment, a sort of determined coolness, which the bending up of my mind to the revenge her crimes deserve, has conferred upon me; I have therefore underlined* some passages in this damned scroll, that my friend may see the weight of that proof on which I proceed. Mark the air of prudery that runs through it, the trick of voluptuous vice to give pleasure the zest of nicety and reluctance. "It may be of guilt." — Mark with what coolness she invites him to participate it! — Is this the handwriting of Julia? — I am awake and see it. — Julia! my wife! damnation!

———

I have been visiting this Lusane, whose house is destined for the scene of my wife's interview with her gallant. I feel the meanness of an inquisition, that degrades me into the wretched spy on an abandoned woman. — I blushed and hesitated while I talked to this old doating minister of their pleasures. But the moment comes when I shall resume myself, when I shall burst upon them in the terrors of punishment.

Whether they have really imposed on the simplicity of this creature, I know not; but her answers to some distant questions of mine looked not like those of an accomplice of their guilt. — Or, rather, it is I who am deceived; the cunning of intrigue is the property of the meanest among the sex — It matters not: I have proof without her.

She conducted me into an inner room fitted up with a degree of nicety. On one side stood a bed, with curtains and a bed-cover of clean cotton. — That bed, Segarva! — but this heart shall down; I will be calm — at the time, while I looked on it, I could not; the

---

* *The passages here alluded to are printed in Italics.*

old woman observed my emotion, and asked if I was ill; I recovered myself, however, and she suspected nothing; I think she did not — It looked as if the beldame had trimmed it for their use — damn her! damn her! killing is poor — canst thou not invent me some luxurious vengeance!

———

Lonquillez has re-sealed, and sent off her letter to Savillon; he will take care to bring me the answer; but I know the answer — "On Monday next," — why should I start as I think on it? — Their fate is fixed! mine perhaps — but I will think no more. Farewell.

———

Rouillé is just arrived here; I could have wished him absent now. He cannot participate my wrongs; they are sacred to more determined souls. Methinks, at this time, I hate his smiles; they suit not the purposes of Montauban.

Julia to Maria

I HOPE, from the conveyance which Lisette has procured for this letter, it may reach you nearly as soon as that in which I inclosed one for Savillon. If it comes in time, let it prevent your delivering that letter. I have been considering of this interview again, and I feel a sort of crime in it towards my husband, which I dare not venture on. I have trespassed too much against sincerity already, in concealing from him my former attachment to that unfortunate young man. So strongly indeed did this idea strike me, that I was preparing to tell it him this very day, when he returned from riding, and found me scarce recovered from the emotion which a re-perusal of Savillon's letter had caused; but his look had a sternness in it, so opposite to those feelings which should have opened the bosom of your distracted Julia, that I shrunk back into secresy, terrified at the reflection on my own purpose. Why am I the wife of this man? but if confidence and tenderness are not mine to give, there is a duty which is not mine to refuse. — Tell Savillon I cannot see him.

Not in the way he asks — let him come as the friend of Julia de Roubigné. Oh, Maria! what a picture do these words recal! the friend of Julia de Roubigné! — in those happy days, when it was not guilt to see, to hear, to think of him — when his poor heart was inconscious of its little wanderings, or felt them but as harmless dreams, which sweetened the real ills of a life too early visited by misfortune!

When I look back on that life, how fateful has it been! Is it unjust in Providence to make this so often the lot of hearts little able to struggle with misfortune? or is it indeed the possession of such hearts that creates their misfortunes? Had I not felt, as I have done, half the ills I complain of had been nothing, and at this moment I were happy. Yet to have wanted such a heart, ill-suited as it is to the rude touch of sublunary things — I think I cannot wish so much. There will come a time, Maria, (might I forebode without your censure, I should say, it may not be distant,) when they shall wound it no longer!

In truth, I am every way weak at present. My poor father adds much to my distresses: he has appeared, for some time past, to be verging towards a state, which alone I should think worse than his death. His affection for me is the only sense now quite alive about him, nay it too partakes of imbecility. He used to embrace me with ardour; he now embraces me with tears.

Judge then, if I am able to meet Savillon at this time, if I could allow myself to meet him at all. Think what I am, and what he is. The coolness I ought to maintain had been difficult at best; at present it is impossible. I can scarce think without weeping; and to see that form —

═══

Maria! when this picture was drawn! — I remember the time well — my father was at Paris, and Savillon left my mother and me at Belville. The painter (who was accidentally in our province) came thither to give me a few lessons of drawing. Savillon was already a tolerable designer; but he joined with me in becoming a scholar to this man. When our master was with us, he used sometimes to guide my hand; when he was gone, at our practice of his instructions, Savillon commonly supplied his place. But Savillon's hand was not like the other's: I felt something from its touch not the less delightful from carrying a sort of fear along with that delight: it was like a pulse in the soul! —

Whither am I wandering? What now are those scenes to me, and why should I wish to remember them? Am I not another's, irrevocably another's? — Savillon knows I am. — Let him not wish to see me: we cannot recal the past, and wherefore, wherefore should we add to the evils of the present?

Montauban to Segarva

I HAVE missed some link of my intelligence; for the day is past, and no answer from Savillon is arrived. I thank him, whatever be the reason; for he has given me time to receive the instructions of my friend.

You caution me well as to the certainty of her guilt. You know the proof I have already acquired; but I will have assurance beyond the possibility of doubt: I will wait their very meeting before I strike this blow, and my vengeance, like that of Heaven, shall be justified by a repetition of her crimes.

I am less easily convinced, or rather I am less willing to be guided, by your opinion, as to the secresy of her punishment. You tell me, that there is but one expiation of a wife's infidelity. — I am resolved, she dies — but that the sacrifice should be secret. Were I even to upbraid her with her crime, you say, her tears, her protestations would outplead the conviction of sense itself, and I should become the dupe of that infamy I am bound to punish. — Is there not something like guilt in this secresy? — Should Montauban shrink, like a coward, from the vindication of his honour? — Should he not burst upon this strumpet and her lover — the picture is beastly — the sword of Montauban! — thou art in the right, it would disgrace it — Let me read your letter again.

═══

I am a fool to be so moved — but your letter has given me back myself. "The disgrace is only published by an open revenge: it can be buried with the guilty by a secret one." — I am yours, Segarva, and you shall guide me.

Chance has been kind to me for the means. Once, in Andalusia, I

met with a Venetian empiric, of whom, among other chemical curi-
osities, I bought a poisonous drug, the efficacy of which he showed
me upon some animals to whom he administered it. The death it
gave was easy, and altered not the appearance of the thing it killed.

───

I have fetched it from my cabinet, and it stands before me. It is
contained in a little square phial, marked with some hieroglyphic
scrawls, which I do not understand. Methinks, while I look on it
— I could be weak, very weak, Segarva — But an hour ago, I saw
her walk, and speak, and smile — yet these few drops! — I will
look on it no more —

I hear the tread of her feet in the apartment above. Did she
know what passes in my mind! — the study in which I sit seems
the cave of a demon!

───

Lonquillez has relieved me again. He has, this moment, got
from her maid the following letter, addressed to her friend
Mademoiselle de Roncilles. What a sex it is! but I have heard of
their alliances of intrigue — It is not that these things are uncommon, but that Montauban is a fool — a husband — a — perdition
seize her!

───

"Is my friend too leagued against me? Alas! my virtue was too
feeble before, and needed not the addition of Maria's arguments to
be overcome. Savillon's figure, you say, aided by that languid
paleness, which his late illness had given it, was irresistible —
Why is not Julia sick? — yet, wretched as she is, irretrievably
wretched, she breathes, and walks, and speaks, as she did in her
most happy days!

"You intreat me, for pity's sake, to meet him. — "He hinted his
design of soon leaving France to return to Martinique." — Why
did he ever leave France? Had he remained contented with love
and Julia, instead of this stolen, this guilty meeting — What do I
say? — I live but for Montauban!

"I will think no longer — This one time I will silence the monitor within me — Tell him I will meet him.[22] On Thursday next, let him be at Lasune's in the evening: it will be dark by six.

"I dare not read what I have written. Farewell."

=====

It will be dark by six! — Yet I will keep my word, Segarva; they shall meet, that certainty may precede my vengeance; but, when they part, they part to meet no more! Lonquillez's fidelity I know: his soul is not that of a servant: he shall provide for Savillon. Julia is a victim above him — Julia shall be the charge of his master.

Farewell! when I write again, it shall not be to threaten.

---

22. That is, her conscience. The formulation is directly derived from Adam Smith's *Theory of Moral Sentiments* where conscience is variously described as an impartial spectator, judge, or 'vice-regent of God' within the breast who scrutinises and pronounces upon the actions of the self. This characteristically Scottish self-division into the potentially antagonistic impulse of actor and observer ultimately derives from the theology of John Calvin.

Savillon to Herbert

AFTER AN interval of torture, I have at last received an answer from Madame de Montauban — Have I lived to write that name! — but it is fit that I be calm.

Her friend has communicated her resolution of allowing me to see her in the house of that good Lasune, whom I have mentioned to you in some of our conversations, as the common nurse of both. Were it not madness to look back, and that, at present, I need the full possession of myself, the idea of Lasune's house would recal such things — but they are past, never, never to return!

━━

I have recovered, and can go on calmly. I set out to-morrow morning: Thursday next is the day she has appointed for our interview. I have but to dispatch this one great business, and then depart from my native country for ever. Every tie that bound me to this world is now broken, except that which accident gave me in your friendship: before I cross the Atlantic, I would once more see my Herbert; when I have indulged myself in that last throb of affection, which our friendship demands at parting, there remains nothing for me to do, but to shrink up from all the feelings of life, and look forward, without emotion, to its close.

━━

I feel, at this moment, as if I were on my death-bed, the necessity of a manly composure; that stifled sigh was the last sacrifice of my weakness! I am now thinking what I have to do with the hours that remain: meet me like a man, and help me to employ them as I ought. Nothing shall drag me back to Europe, and therefore I would shake off every occasion to revisit it.

Though the externals of place and distance are not of much importance to me, yet there is something in large towns that I wish to avoid. As you mention a design of being in Dorsetshire sometime soon, may I ask you to make next week that time, and meet me at the town of Pool[23] in that county? Inconsiderable and unknown as I am, there are circumstances that might mark me out in Picardy; and therefore I shall go by Dieppe to that port of England, where I know I shall, at this season, find an opportunity of getting over the Atlantic.

I inclose a letter to a merchant in London, relating to some business, in which my uncle was concerned, with the house of which he is a partner. Be so kind to forward it, and let him know that I desire the answer may be committed to your care. As I see by his correspondence, that he is not altogether a man of business, he may perhaps be desirous of meeting with you, to ask some questions about the nephew of his old acquaintance. He will wonder, as others will, at so rich a man returning to Martinique. If a reason is necessary, invent some one; it is peculiar to misery like mine to be incapable of being told. — I shall relapse, if I continue to write. — You will, if it is possible, meet me at Pool; if not, write to me thither, where I shall find you. Let your letter wait me at the post-house. Farewell.

23. Poole, in Dorset, England.

Julia to Maria

THE HOUR is almost arrived! My husband has just left me: he came into my room in his riding dress. — "I shall not be at home," said he, "till supper-time, and Rouillé's shooting party will detain him till it is late." — The consciousness of my purpose pressed upon my tongue while I answered him: I faltered, and could hardly speak. "You speak faintly," said Montauban. "You are not ill, I hope," taking my hand. I told him, truly, that my head ached a good deal, that it had ached all day, that I meant to try if a walk would do it service. "Perhaps it may," answerd he; and methought he looked steadily, and with a sort of question at me; or rather my own mind interpreted his look in that manner — I believe I blushed —

How I tremble as I look on my watch! Would I could recal my promise.

———

I am somewhat bolder now; but it is not from having conquered my fear; something like despair assists me. — It wants but a few minutes — the hand that points them seems to speak as I watch it. — I come, Savillon, I come!

———

How shall I describe our meeting? I am unfit for describing — it cannot be described — I shall be calmer by and bye.

———

I know not how I got to the house. From the moment I quitted my chamber, I was unconscious of every thing around me. The first object that struck my eye was Savillon; I recollect my nurse

placing me in a chair opposite to where he sat — she left us — I felt
the room turning round with me — I had fainted, it seems. When
I recovered, I found her supporting me in her arms, and holding a
phial of salts to my nose. Savillon had my hands in his, gazing on
me with a countenance of distress and terror. My eye met his, and,
for some moments, I looked on him, as I have done in my dreams,
unmindful of our situation. The pressure of his hand awakened
me to recollection. He looked on me more earnestly still, and
breathed out the word Julia! — It was all he could utter; but it
spoke such things, Maria! — You cannot understand its force.
Had you felt it as I did! — I could not, indeed I could not, help
bursting into tears.

"My dearest children," cried the good Lasune, taking our
hands, which were still folded together, and squeezing them in
her's. The action had something of that tender simplicity in it,
which is not to be resisted. I wept afresh; but my tears were less
painful than before.

She fetched a bottle of wine from a cupboard, and forced me to
take a glass of it. She offered another to Savillon. He put it by,
with a gentle inclination of his head. "You shall drink it, indeed,
my dear boy," she said; "it is a long time since you tasted any thing
in this house." He gave a deep sigh, and drank it.

She had given us time to recover the power of speech: but I
knew less how to begin speaking than before. My eyes now found
something in Savillon's which they were ashamed to meet. Lasune
left us; I almost wished her to stay.

Savillon sat down in his former place; he threw his eyes on the
ground — "I know not," said he, in a faltering voice, "how to
thank you for the condescension of this interview — our former
friendship" I trembled for what he seemed about to say. — "I
have not forgotten it," said I, half interrupting him. — I saw him
start from his former posture, as if awaked by the sound of my
voice. — "I ask not," continued he, "to be remembered: I am
unworthy of your remembrance — In a short time, I shall be a
voluntary exile from France, and breathe out the remains of life

amidst a race of strangers, who cannot call forth those affections, that would henceforth be shut to the world!" — "Speak not thus!" I cried, "for pity's sake, speak not thus! Live, and be happy, happy as your virtues deserve, as Julia wishes you!" — "Julia wish me happy!" — "Oh, Savillon, you know not the heart that you wring thus! — If it has wronged you, you are revenged enough. — "Revenged! revenged on Julia! Heaven is my witness, I intreated this meeting, that my parting words might bless her!" — He fell on his knees before me — "May that power," he cried, "who formed this excellence, reward it! May every blessing this life can bestow, be the portion of Julia! May she be happy, long after the tongue that asks it is silent for ever, and the heart that now throbs with the wish, has ceased its throbbing!" — Had you seen him, Maria, as he uttered this! — What should I have done? — Weeping, trembling, unconscious, as it were, of myself, I spoke I know not what — told him the weakness of my soul, and lamented the destiny that made me another's. This was too much. When I could recollect myself, I felt that it was too much. I would have retracted what I had said: I spoke of the duty I owed to Montauban, of the esteem which his virtues deserved. — "I have heard of his worth," said Savillon; "I needed no proof to be convinced of it; he is the husband of Julia." — There was something in the tone of these last words, that undid my resolution again. — I told him of the false intelligence I had received of his marriage, without which no argument of prudence, no partial influence, could have made me the wife of another. He put his hand to his heart, and threw his eyes wildly to heaven. — I shrunk back at that look of despair, which his countenance assumed. He took two or three hurried turns through the room; then resuming his seat, and lowering his voice, "It is enough," said he, "I am fated to be miserable! but the contagion of my destiny shall spread no farther. This night I leave France for ever!" — "This night!" I exclaimed. "It must be so," said he, with a determined calmness; "but before I go, let me deposit in your hands this paper. It is a memorial of that Savillon, who was the friend of Julia! — I opened it: it was a will, bequeathing his fortune to me. "This must not be," said I, "this must not be. — Think not, I conjure you, so despairingly of life; live to enjoy that fortune, which is so seldom the reward of merit like thine. I have no title to its disposal." — "You have the best one," returned Savillon, still preserving his composure; "I never valued wealth, but as it might render me, in the language of the world, more worthy of thee. To make it thine, was the purpose of my wishing to acquire it; to make it thine is still in my power." — "I cannot receive this, indeed I cannot. Think of the situation in which I stand." I pressed the paper upon him: he took it at last, and pausing, as if he thought, for a moment — "You are right; there may be an impropriety in your keeping it. — Alas! I have scarce a friend, to whom I can entrust any thing; yet I may find one, who will see it faithfully executed."

He was interrupted by Lasune, who entered somewhat hurriedly, and told me, Lisette was come to fetch me, and that she had met my husband in her way to the house. "We must part then," said he, "for ever! — let not a thought of the unfortunate Savillon disturb the happiness which Heaven allots to Julia; she shall hear of him but once again — when that period arrives, it will not offend the happy Montauban, if she drops a tear to the memory of one, whose love was expiated by his sufferings!" — Maria! was it a breach of virtue, if then I threw myself on his neck, if then I wept on his bosom? His look, his last look! I see it still! never shall I forget it! —

Merciful God! at whose altar I vowed fidelity to another! impute not to me as a crime the remembrance of Savillon! — thou canst see the purity of that heart which bleeds at the remembrance!

———

Eleven at night.

You know my presentiments of evil; never did I feel them so strong as at present. I tremble to go to bed — the taper that burns by me is dim, and methinks my bed looks like a grave!

━━

I was weak enough to call back Lisette. I pretended some little business for her; the poor girl observed that I looked ill, and asked if she should sit by me? I had almost said, Yes; but had courage enough to combat my fears in that instance. She bid me Good-night — there was somewhat solemn in her utterance of that "good-night"; I fancy mine was not without its particular emphasis, for she looked back wistfully as I spoke. —

I will say my prayers, and forget it; pray for me too, my friend. I have need of your prayers, indeed I have — Good night to my dearest Maria!

━━

If I have recollection enough — Oh! my Maria — I will be calm — it was but a dream — will you blush for my weakness? Yet hear me — if this should be the last time I shall ever write — the memory of my friend mingles with the thought! — yet methinks I could, at this time, beyond any other, die contented.

My fears had given way to sleep; but their impression was on my fancy still. Methought I sat in our family monument at Belville, with a single glimmering lamp, that showed the horrors of the place, when, on a sudden, a light, like that of the morning, burst on the gloomy vault, and the venerable figures of my fathers, such as I had seen them in the pictures of our hall, stood smiling benignity upon me! The attitude of the foremost was that of attention, his finger resting upon his lip. — I listened; when sounds of more than terrestrial melody stole upon my ear, borne, as it were, upon the distant wind, till they swelled at last to music so exquisite, that my ravished sense was stretched too far for delusion, and I awoke in the midst of the entrancement!

I rose, with the memory of the sounds full upon my mind; the candle I had ordered to stand by me was still unextinguished. I sat down to the organ, and, with that small soft stop you used to call seraphic, endeavoured to imitate their beauty. And never before did your Julia play an air so heavenly, or feel such extacy in the power of sound! When I had catched the solemn chord that last arose in my dream, my fingers dwelt involuntarily on the keys, and methought I saw the guardian spirits around me, listening with a rapture like mine! —

But it will not last — the blissful delusion is gone, and I am left a weak and unhappy woman still! —

I am sick at heart, Maria, and a faintness like that of death —

=====

The fit is over, and I am able to write again; and I will write while I am able. Methinks, my friend, I am taking farewell of you, and I would lengthen out the lingering words as much as I can. I am just now recalling the scenes of peaceful happiness we have enjoyed together. — I imagine I feel the arm of my Maria thrown round my neck — her tears fall on my bosom! — Think of me when I am gone. — This faintness again! — Farewell! farewell! perhaps —

Montauban to Segarva

IT IS done, Segarva, it is done; the poor unthinking — Support me, my friend, support me with the thoughts of that vengeance I owe to my honour — the guilty Julia has a few hours to live.

—

I did but listen a moment at the door; I thought I heard her maid upon the stairs — it is not yet the time. — Hark! it was not my wife's bell — the clock struck eleven — never shall she hear it strike that hour again!

Pardon me, my Segarva; methinks I speak to you, when I scrawl upon this paper. I wish for somebody to speak to; to answer, to comfort, to guide me!

Had you seen her, when these trembling hands delivered her the bowl! — She had complained of being ill, and begged to lie alone; but her illness seemed of the mind, and, when she spoke to me, she betrayed the embarrassment of guilt. I gave her the drug as a cordial. She took it from me, smiling, and her look seemed to lose its confusion. She drank my health! She was dressed in a white silk bed-gown, ornamented with pale pink ribbands. Her cheek was gently flushed from their reflection; her blue eyes were turned upwards as she drank, and a dark brown ringlet lay on her shoulder. Methinks I see her now — how like an angel she looked! Had she been innocent, Segarva! — You know, you know, it is impossible she can be innocent.

—

Let me recollect myself — a man, a soldier, a friend of Segarva! —

At the word *innocent* I stopped; I could scarce hold my pen; I rose from my seat, I know not why. Methought some one passed behind me in the room. I snatched up my sword in one hand, and a candle in the other. It was my own figure in a mirror that stood at my back. — What a look was mine! — Am I a murderer? — Justice cannot murder, and the vengeance of Montauban is just.

====

Lonquillez has been with me — I durst not question him when he entered the apartment — but the deed is not done; he could not find Savillon. After watching for several hours, he met a peasant, whom he had seen attending him the day before, who informed him, that the strange gentleman had set off, some time after it grew dark, in a post-chaise, which drove away at full speed. Is my revenge then incomplete? or is one victim sufficient to the injured honour of a husband? — What a victim is that one!

I went down stairs to let Lonquillez out by a private passage, of which I keep the key. When I was returning to my apartment, I heard the sound of music proceeding from my wife's chamber: — there is a double door on it; I opened the outer one without any noise, and the inner has some panes of glass at top, through which I saw part of the room. Segarva! she sat at the organ, her fingers pressing on the keys, and her look up-raised with enthusiastic rapture! — the solemn sounds still ring in my ear! such as angels might play, when the sainted soul ascends to heaven! — I am the fool of appearances, when I have such proofs — Lisette is at my door.

====

It is now that I feel myself a coward; the horrid draught has begun to operate! She thinks herself in danger; a physician is sent for, but he lives at a distance; before he arrives — Oh, Segarva!

====

She begged I would quit the chamber; she saw my confusion, and thought it proceeded from distress at her illness. — Can guilt be thus mistress of herself? — let me not think that way — my brain is too weak for it! — Lisette again!

═══

She is guilty, and I am not a murderer! I go to —

Monsieur de Rouillé to Mademoiselle de Roncilles

MADAM,

THE WRITER of this letter has no title to address you, except that which common friendship, and common calamity, may give him.

Amidst the fatal scenes, which he has lately witnessed, his recollection was lost; when it returned, it spoke of Mademoiselle de Roncilles, the first, he believes, and dearest friend of the most amiable but most unfortunate Madame de Montauban. The office he now undertakes is terrible; but it is necessary. — You must soon be told, that your excellent friend is no more! Hear it then from one, who knew her excellence, as you did; who tells the horrid circumstances of her death with a bleeding heart. — Yes, Madam, I must prepare you for horrors; and, while the remembrance tears my own bosom, assume the calmness that is necessary for yours.

On the evening of Thursday last, I was told Madame de Montauban was a good deal indisposed, and had gone to bed before her usual time. At a very short and silent supper, I perceived her husband uncommonly agitated, and, as soon as decency would allow me, withdrew and left him. Betwixt eleven and twelve o'clock, (I had not yet gone to bed,) one of the maid-servants came to my room, begging I would instantly attend her to the chamber of her mistress, who was so extremely ill, that, without immediate assistance, they feared the very worst consequences. I had formerly a little knowledge of physic, and had been in use to practise it in some particular campaigns, when abler hands could not be had. I ran down stairs with the servant, desiring my own man to seek out a little case of lancets, and follow us. The girl informed her mistress of my being at the door of her apartment. She desired I might come in, and with that smile, which sickness could not quench, stretched out her hand to me. I found her pulse low and weak, and she complained of a strange fluttering at her heart, which hardly allowed her to speak. I was afraid to venture on bleeding, and only gave her a little of some common restoratives, that were at hand. She found herself somewhat relieved, and sat up in her bed, supported by her maid. Montauban entered the room. His countenance surprised me; it was not that of distress alone, it was marked with turbulence and horror. It seemed to hurt his wife. At that moment she was scarce able to speak; but she forced out a few broken words, begging him to leave the room, for that her illness affected him too much. He withdrew in silence. In a little time, she seemed a good deal easier; but her pulse was still lower than before. She ordered her maid to call Mons. de Montauban again: "I dare not trust to future moments," said she, "and I have something important to reveal to him." — I offered to leave the room as he entered. — "His friend may hear it," she said, in a faultering voice. She fixed her eye languidly, but steadily, on Montauban. He advanced towards her with an eager gaze, without uttering a word. When she would have spoken, her voice failed her again; and she beckoned, but with a modesty in her action, signifying her desire that he should sit down by her. She took his hand; he seemed unconscious of her taking it, and continued to bend a look of earnestness upon her.

When she had recovered the power of utterance, "I feel, Sir," said she, "something in this illness predictive of the worst; at any rate, I would prepare for it. If I am now to die, I hope (lifting up her eyes with a certain meek assurance which it is impossible to paint) I die in peace with heaven! There is one account which I wish to settle with you: these moments of ease, which I enjoy, are allowed me to confess my offence, and entreat your forgiveness."

"Thou wert guilty then!" exclaimed her husband, starting from his seat. She paused in astonishment at the impassioned gesture he assumed — "Speak!" cried Montauban, recovering himself a little, his voice suffocated with the word.

"When you have heard me," said Julia, "you will find I am less guilty than unfortunate; yet I am not innocent, for then I should not have been the wife of Montauban.

"When I became yours, my heart owned you not for the lord of its affections; there was an attachment — Yet look not so sternly on me! — he in whose favour that possession was formed, would not have wronged you, if he could. His virtues were the objects of my affection; and had Savillon been the thing you fear, Julia had been guiltless even of loving him in secret. — Till yesterday, he never told me his love; till yesterday, he knew not I had ever loved him." —

"But yesterday!" — cried Montauban, seeming to check the agitation he had shown before, and lowering his voice into a tone of calm severity.

"For the offence of yesterday," said she, "I would obtain your pardon, and die in peace. I met Savillon in secret; I saw the anguish in his soul, and pitied it. Was it a crime thus to meet him? Was it a crime to confess my love, while I received the last farewell of the unfortunate Savillon? — This is my offence; — perhaps the last that Julia can commit, or you forgive!"

He clasped his hands convulsively together, and throwing up to heaven a look of despair, fell senseless into my arms. Julia would have sprung to his assistance, but her strength was unequal to the effort; her maid screamed for help, and several of the servants rushed into the room. We recovered the hapless Montauban; he looked round wildly for a moment, then fastening his eyes on Julia, — "I have murdered thee!" he cried: "That draught I gave thee — that draught was death!" He would have pressed her to his bosom; she sunk from his embrace — her closing eye looked piteous upon him — her hand was half stretched to his — and a single sigh breathed out her soul to heaven!

"She shall not die," he cried, eagerly catching hold of her hand, and bending over her lifeless body with a glare of inconceivable horror in his aspect. I laid hold of his arm, endeavouring to draw his attention towards me; but he seemed not to regard me, and continued that frightful gaze upon the remains of his much injured wife. I made a sign for the servants to assist me, and, taking his hand, began to use a gentle sort of violence, to lead him away. He started back a few paces, without, however, altering the direction of his eye. "You may torture me," cried he, wildly, "I can bear it all — Ha! Segarva there! — let them prove the hand-writing if they can — mark it, I say there is no blood in her face — let me ask one question at the doctor — you know the effects of poison — her lips are white — bid Savillon kiss them now — they shall speak no more — Julia shall speak no more!"

Word was now brought me, that the physician, who had been sent for to the assistance of Julia, was arrived. He had come, alas! too late for her; but I meant to use his skill on behalf of Montauban. I repeated my endeavours to get him away from the dreadful object before him; and, at last, though he seemed not to heed the entreaties I made use of, he allowed himself to be conducted to his own apartment, where the doctor was in waiting. There were marks of confusion in this man's countenance, which I wished to dissipate. I made use of some expressive looks, to signify that he should appear more easy; and, assuming that manner myself, begged Montauban to allow him to feel his pulse. — "You come to see my wife," said he, turning towards him, — "tread softly — she will do well enough when she wakes. There!" stretching out his arm, — "your hand trembles sadly; I will count the beatings myself — here is something amiss; but I am not mad. — Your name is Arpentier, mine is Montauban — I am not mad." — The physician desired him to get undressed, and go to bed. "I mean to do so, for I have not slept these two nights — but it is better not. Give me some potion against bad dreams — that's well thought on — that's well thought on."

His servant had begun to undress him. He went for a few minutes into his closet; he returned with his night-gown on, and his look appeared more thoughtful, and less wild than formerly.

He made a slight bow to the physician: — "I shall see you when I rise, Sir. — Rouillé, is it not?" addressing himself to me, and squeezing my hand — "I am not fit for talking just now, I know I am not — Good night!" I left him, whispering his servant to stay in the room, unperceived, if he could; but at any rate, not to leave his master alone.

I know not how I was so long able to command reflection. The moment I left Montauban, the horror of the scene I had witnessed rushed upon my mind, and I remember nothing of what passed, till I found myself kneeling before the breathless remains of the ill-fated Julia. The doctor was standing by me, with a letter in his hand: it was written by Montauban, and had been found open on the table of his study. Arpentier gave it me, saying, it contained things which should be communicated only to the friends of the count. From it I discovered the dreadful certainty of what I had before gathered from the distracted words of Montauban. He had supposed his wife faithless, his bed dishonoured, and had revenged the imagined injury by poison. — My God! I can scarce, at this moment, believe that I have waked and seen this!

But his servant now came running into the room, calling for us to hasten into his master's chamber, for that he feared he was dead. We rushed into the room together — it was too true: Montauban was no more! The doctor tried, he confessed without hope, several expedients to revive him; but they failed of success. I hung over the bed, entranced in the recollection of the fateful events I had seen. Arpentier, from the habit of looking on the forms of death, was more master of himself; after examining the body, and pondering a little on the behaviour of the count, he went into the closet, where he found, on a small table, a phial uncorked, which he brought to me. It explained the fate of Montauban; a label fastened to it, was inscribed LAUDANUM; its deadly contents he had swallowed in his delirium before he went to bed.

Such was the conclusion of a life distinguished by the exercise of every manly virtue; and, except in this instance, unstained by a crime. While I mourn the fate of his most amiable wife, I recal the memory of my once dearly-valued friend, and would shelter it with some apology if I could. Let that honour which he worshipped plead in his defence. — That honour we have worshipped together, and I would not weaken its sacred voice; but I look on the body of Montauban — I weep over the pale corpse of Julia! — I shudder at the sacrifices of mistaken honour, and lift up my hands to pity and to justice.

* * * * * * *